BACKWARD GLANCES

Wendy Haskett

Copyright © 2002 by Wendy Haskett

All rights reserved. No part of this book shall be reproduced or transmitted in any form or by any means, electronic, mechanical, magnetic, photographic including photocopying, recording or by any information storage and retrieval system, without prior written permission of the publisher. No patent liability is assumed with respect to the use of the information contained herein. Although every precaution has been taken in the preparation of this book, the publisher and author assume no responsibility for errors or omissions. Neither is any liability assumed for damages resulting from the use of the information contained herein.

This is a work of fiction. Names, characters, places, and incidents either are the product of the author's imagination or are used fictitiously. Any resemblance to actual events or locales or persons, living or dead, is entirely coincidental.

ISBN 0-7414-1056-7

Published by:

Infinity Publishing.com
519 West Lancaster Avenue
Haverford, PA 19041-1413
Info@buybooksontheweb.com
www.buybooksontheweb.com
Toll-free (877) BUY BOOK
Local Phone (610) 520-2500
Fax (610) 519-0261

Printed in the United States of America
Printed on Recycled Paper
Published March, 2002

"There is no street with mute stones,
and no house without echoes,"
--Gongora

For Scotty

Table of Contents

CHAPTER ONE
"Growing Up Before There Were Freeways" 1

CHAPTER TWO
"North County Bars Ranged from Sophisticated to Rowdy" 5

CHAPTER THREE
"Doctor Practices in Medicine's 'Golden Years'" 9

CHAPTER FOUR
"Green Valley School, Floods, Goats and Mr. Loveless" 13

CHAPTER FIVE
"Fletcher Cove's Lifeguards Thanked with Cookies, $100 Bills" 17

CHAPTER SIX
"Leaving Cardiff-By-The-Sea" 21

CHAPTER SEVEN
"Amelia's Wedding Gift" 25

CHAPTER EIGHT
"Christiana, Portrait of a Pioneer." 29

CHAPTER NINE
"Eden Garden's Pool-playing Twins" 33

CHAPTER TEN
  "VG Donuts"... 37

CHAPTER ELEVEN
  "Aladdin's Cave--The Wilkens Wonderful Store"...................................... 41

CHAPTER TWELVE
  "Tak Sugimoto--Going Home to Encinitas "... 45

CHAPTER THIRTEEN
  "Sid Shaw and the Riffraff Boys""... 50

CHAPTER FOURTEEN
  "The Kickapoos' Giant Kite "... 54

CHAPTER FIFTEEN
  "The Colorful Jobs of Ernie Bertoncini"... 58

CHAPTER SIXTEEN
  " Captain Kenos ".. 62

CHAPTER SEVENTEEN
  "George Bumann, Advice Remembered From a Pioneer Father."............. 66

CHAPTER EIGHTEEN
  "Three Generations of McIntires Worked At Racetrack"........................... 70

CHAPTER NINETEEN
  "Dr. Harry Hill, First Encinitas Vet to Open Small Animal Practice"....... 74

CHAPTER TWENTY
  "Floods, Coyotes, and Amorous Turkeys"... 78

CHAPTER TWENTY ONE
"King Brothers' Business began in Back Yard Shed" 82

CHAPTER TWENTY TWO
"Olivenhain's Pioneer Cemetery" 86

CHAPTER TWENTY THREE
"The Danforth Building" 90

CHAPTER TWENTY FOUR
"Herman Wiegand and The Talking Machine " 94

CHAPTER TWENTY FIVE
" When The North County Waited For An Enemy Invasion" 98

CHAPTER TWENTY SIX
"Bill Arballo" 103

CHAPTER TWENTY SEVEN
The Rupe Family, Weathering Ups & Downs in early Encinitas" 107

CHAPTER TWENTY EIGHT
"The King's Men" 111

CHAPTER TWENTY NINE
"Drugstore Soda Fountains Once Gathering Places" 115

CHAPTER THIRTY
"Pines, Spaghetti and Puddles Part of Cardiff School's History" 119

CHAPTER THIRTY ONE
" Terrace Rats Stick With Traditional Tattoo" 123

CHAPTER THIRTY TWO
    "A Fascination With the Past Leads Cardiff Couple into Adventures" ... 127

CHAPTER THIRTY THREE
    "Lyle Hammond, the Irresistible Eagle Beak" 131

CHAPTER THIRTY FOUR
    "Using Up the Leftovers" 135

CHAPTER THIRTY FIVE
    "Movie Stars Most Visible in Old Del Mar" 139

CHAPTER THIRTY SIX
    "The Friendly Dalagers" 143

CHAPTER THIRTY SEVEN
    "The Terwilliger Family, Horses, Dancing and Del Mar Roots" 147

CHAPTER THIRTY EIGHT
    "Four Presley Brothers Remembered with Affection" 151

CHAPTER THIRTY NINE
    "Lauralie Dunne Stanton, growing Up Next-door to Auntie Bath." 155

CHAPTER FORTY
    "Cory's Mercantile" 159

CHAPTER FORTY ONE
    "Maggie Zuerner Wolfe--a Life Filled With Firsts." 163

CHAPTER FORTY TWO
    "Moonlight Beach Scene of Picnics, Parties and Laundry" 167

CHAPTER FORTY THREE
 "Lima beans, Dust, Played Role in 1930s Romance" 171

CHAPTER FORTY FOUR
 "Lucky Jack and his Fishing Family" 175

CHAPTER FORTY FIVE
 "Growing Up in Eden Gardens" 179

CHAPTER FORTY SIX
 "Blimps" 183

FORTY SEVEN
 "Jay Harold and Babe On the Saturday-Crowded Sidewalk" 187

CHAPTER FORTY EIGHT
 "Lola's Double Life" 191

CHAPTER FORTY NINE
 "The Coles of Cole Ranch Road" 196

CHAPTER FIFTY
 "Visitors Survive Strong Dose of North County History" 200

INTRODUCTION

"The personalities of the people I interviewed became a part of my life. They'll always be with me. Everyone taught me something."
—Maura Wiegand Harvey, author of "San Dieguito Heritage."

"Would you like to write a history column for us?" Teresa Hineline asked me. A long, blonde braid swung over one of her shoulders. Her office, on Solana Beach's Cedros Avenue, rattled every time a train roared past.

It was January 1998, and Teresa, at that time, was city editor of the North County Times' Encinitas Zone.

"You could look back at the histories of Leucadia, Encinitas, Cardiff, Solana Beach, Del Mar and Olivenhain," she suggested. "A weekly column."

A weekly column?

I drove home wondering how I was ever going to come up with enough "history" to keep it chugging along. The North County, to me, seemed so new!

Part of my childhood had been spent in Britain's ancient city of Chester--where the grooves on top of the city's walls got their start in the 5th century from the sandals of patrolling Romans.

On holidays in Ireland my family had picnics beside a Druid stone that was supposed to have been around when Saint Patrick was trying to convert Pagans to Christianity. (The Pagans were rather unsporting about this, and used to set their dogs on him.)

By contrast, when the Mackinnons, the first family to settle in Cardiff, built their ranch house in 1874 the only sign of other settlers having been there was a baby's grave.

What I discovered, though, is that North County's history comes through its people. It's rich in people with spirit and imagination. People who got things done and who were either interesting, or eccentric, or inspiring, or all three.

The pioneer spirit flourished here. It still does.

In this collection of fifty columns I've left out some that are absolute favorites of mine. This is because I'm planning four "Backward Glance" books, (at least), and felt they would be more entertaining if the chapters had a lot of variety.

One of my MiraCosta College writing students, Dorothy Jensen, has a saying, "God willing, and the creek don't rise." God willing and the creek don't rise, the next three "Backward Glance" books after this one are scheduled for Fall 2002, Spring 2003 and Fall 2003.

Some of the people in this book have died since I plucked up their memories. To their families, their friends, I'd like to say how glad I am that I was able to meet them. Actually, I'm not just glad, I'm delighted!

Wendy Haskett,
April 2002

CHAPTER ONE

Growing Up Before There Were Freeways"

Written May 2000

    I think of them as the boys of summer; those boys born in the years between the world wars when this area was full of wide open spaces. They were rich if they had a bicycle, a slingshot, and a dime to see action-packed movies like "Lives of the Bengal Lancers".

In the 1930s the creek below the bridge on Rancho Santa Fe Road teamed with so many crawdads, Bluegill perch and catfish that barefoot kids toted them home in bucketfuls.

In downtown Encinitas the traffic was so sparse that Ed Cory remembers playing baseball in the street outside his dad's clothing store--right on Highway 101, between D and E Streets.

"We'd put a kid at the Shell station on the corner to watch and holler if a car was coming," he said. "Sometimes we'd get a whole game in before we had to pick up our stuff and scramble."

No one in the area owned a proper surfboard, he said. "We just body-surfed. Once, when I was in Junior High, I won a surfing contest sponsored by Ivan Tiedy, owner of the town's appliance store. The first prize was an ironing board, which was kind of disappointing. I lugged it home and said, 'Here, Mom, you can have it!'"

Those were the days when Encinitas "City Kids", (meaning they lived west of the railroad tracks), hunkered near the tennis courts at Moonlight Beach to play marble tournaments against "Country Kids".

Fireworks were legal then.

"Every 4th of July we used to set off firecrackers topped by tuna cans," remembers Jay Harold Williams, who grew up in Cardiff. "We put them under lamp posts because the goal was to see if you could blow them as high as the lights."

Slingshots, firing everything from castor beans to smaller-than-a-marble iron oxide stones found in a ravine behind Quail Gardens, were a vital piece of "boy equipment". Kids often made their own from inner tubes. "Or they used the type David used on Goliath," Tak Sugimoto said. "You took a thick cord and slung it around your head."

All of the boys of summer swam, and not only at the beach. (Every time I pass the lake near the edge of the golf course on Leucadia Boulevard I think of Bob Grice rising from it covered with leeches. "They didn't bother me at all," he said.)

Tak Sugimoto actually created a swimming hole for his friends one summer while his parents were away. "There was an empty water tank on the edge of our farmland on Saxony Road," he said. "I filled it with water--gallons and gallons and gallons of water. Then, for authenticity, I poured in some crawdads and Bluegill perch."

His parents, he remembers, were appalled when they saw their water bill. "It was astronomical. My father tried to use the water to irrigate his strawberry fields, but the fish kept blocking up the pipes."

Del Mar was such a small town in the late '30s that Don Terwilliger was able to get away with swinging from Monterey Cyprus trees along Ocean Avenue while pretending to be Tarzan. (Some of those trees are still there.)

"We used to ride horses along the beach," he said. "One whole block of Del Mar, between 19th and 18th Streets, was a fenced in corral where people kept their horses. It was owned by the Crabtrees."

From about age six Don always had a horse of some kind, he said, because his grandfather, Claude Terwilliger, was a horse trader.

"Among many other things," he said of his entrepreneurial grandfather, who was one of Rancho Santa Fe's earliest residents. Claude believed that business was business and would sell the family's horses, including his wife's, if offered a good enough price. As well as horses, he provided Don with several mules and a Shetland pony that refused to go further than one block.

"The most unusual animal he gave me was a white burrow," Don said." Grandfather paid $15 for a black donkey, bred her to a brown and white one, and their offspring, named Toby, was so white he looked like a rabbit. I loved Toby. It nearly killed me when Grandfather sold him to a dude ranch for $150."

In the '30s a typical North County boy milked at least one cow, or the family goat, before school. He could--and did--drive his dad's car by age ten and was a crack shot with a hunting rifle. One thing that hasn't changed, though, is boys' love of zooming on skateboards.

"Ours were scooter-skateboards. They usually had a handle in front," Jay Harold Williams said. "We made our own, using wheels from roller skates."

"We drove the downtown Encinitas merchants crazy," Tak Sugimoto remembers. "In the '30s that stretch along 101 was the only part of the area with sidewalks."

CHAPTER TWO

"North County Bars Ranged from Sophisticated to Rowdy"

Written December 1999

A few days after this column appeared in the newspaper I got a phone call from a woman with a gentle voice. Fifty years ago, she told me, she'd worked in Leucadia as a cleaner at Ruby's bar.

"It was, um, you know, one of those places....." she said.
"One of those places?"
"Oh, you know, dear...a house of ill repute."

When he first saw Leucadia, in 1946, 21-year-old professional boxer John Kentera thought it was a small, quiet town. It seemed vastly different from the glitter of Reno, Nevada, where, between fights, he was earning good extra money working as a bartender But by the '50s, when he was running his own bar, The Leucadian, on Highway 101, John knew that the town may have been small but it was filled with interesting people.

People like the late Ruby Nelson, of Ruby's Bar. (It stood where Royal Liquors is now.)

"Ruby was a big, buxom woman, who smoked Crook's rum-soaked cigars. She had a heart as large as a watermelon, but if a male customer sassed her she'd smack him on the head with a broom," John said. "Ruby had an on-going feud with the local sheriff, Charlie McIntire, over having dancing there without a dance license. If the customers saw the sheriff coming, someone would flip a breaker switch and plunge the bar into darkness."

John first traveled to Leucadia from Reno to help his parents when they opened a grocery store, The Palace Market, in the 1500 block of North 101. For several years he moved back and forth, winning, in 1949, Nevada's State heavyweight Boxing Championship in 1949.

"I won it from Jitterbug Collier on a decision," he said. "But lost it in the rematch when he knocked me out."

In Leucadia John worked days in the family market, and nights at local bar-and-restaurants along 101, including Vienna Villa (where Captain Keno's is now) and Cardiff's Beacon Inn (torn down years ago).

The Beacon Inn was on the beach and, he said, as lively as anything in Reno. "They had the best food in the area, a dance floor and burlesque with beautiful show girls. Two shows a night, at nine and eleven. The place was always packed."

Around 1950 the owner, Ray McCullough, sold the Beacon Inn and John went to work at The Del Mar Hotel (another landmark building since torn down). That year the hotel was feeding around a thousand people a night and employed fifty waiters, fifteen cocktail waitresses and seven bartenders. Their stage shows, featuring performers such as Nat King Cole and Liberace, were so popular, John remembers, "That even with two shows a night many people couldn't get in the door."

Every racing season, he said, the hotel buzzed with movie stars and top jockeys, with guests as diverse as Betty Grable and Willie Shoemaker and Lou Costello, whose round face--"His eyes grew rounder with every drink"--made people smile even before he said anything.

"Rex Coleman, who worked in Del Mar's post office, played piano in the bar at night. Jimmy Durante used to tell him, "Take a couple of hours off, kid. I'll pay for your drinks," and then he'd sit down at Rex's piano and play."

"One time, when the assistant manager and his wife had been in a car accident and couldn't pay their medical bills, Jimmy Durante said, 'Come on folks, gotta make some money for this couple.' He played for hours while somebody passed around that dun-colored fedora hat he always wore. The hat ended up stuffed with fifty and one hundred dollar bills."

In 1954 John, with his brother Andy, opened The Leucadian. Their parents had retired by then, so The Palace Market was knocked down to become the bar's parking lot. (It still is.)

In those days, John said, there wasn't a regular fire department; instead fires were put out mostly by volunteers. "A call would come into the bar saying there was a fire and asking if any volunteer firemen were there. There were usually several of them there, eating dinner because the bar served food. They'd leap up from their meals and dash off to fight the fire in whatever they were wearing, which was sometimes a suit."

The local pharmacist, Roy Blackburn, Sr., also would leave his dinner and go and prepare a prescription--"Even at ten at night," John said --if a needy customer came looking for him. But local residents weren't angels. John admits they had a little fun in the bar kidding tourists.

"One time a local fisherman, Stan Lewis, sold me eighteen lobsters, "shorts", for fifty cents each. A tourist from Idaho overheard me telling locals that I'd just caught all eighteen in the surf. He didn't realize this was impossible."

The man, John said, went over to Value Fair (a Cardiff store much loved in the 60s and 70s because it carried practically everything) and bought a fishing rod.

"Next day he was back. He could barely speak. As I fixed him hot whiskey with honey he croaked that he'd been out all night surf fishing and hadn't caught a single lobster. I felt so guilty I gave him all eighteen of Stan's."

In 1975 John's brother-in-law, Jack Carney, died. Jack had been a partner in the Cardiff bar "The Office", and John and Andy took over from him, traveling back and forth between the two bars (both of which still have photographs of John in his boxing days behind the bar).

John retired in 1993, but years before that he encountered Ruby, of Ruby's Bar, in Value Fair.

"She was plainly dressed, wearing no make-up. 'Ruby?' I said.' Is that you?' She told me she'd become religious, had quit smoking the rum soaked cigars, and was now teaching Sunday School."

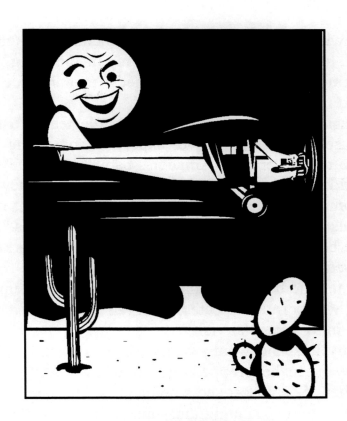

CHAPTER THREE

"Doctor Practices in Medicine's 'Golden Years'"

Written January 2000

    On a warm August day in 1948 Fred Brass, a 27-year-old medical doctor, set out to visit the other doctors in his area. "To let them know I was starting my own practice the next day," he said. "That was considered good medical ethics."

Dr. Novak, who practiced in downtown Encinitas, asked Fred if he'd go out on a house call, he remembers. "Here, take my medical bag," he said, handing me a battered-looking one. "It's a family named Amador. Nice people. Husband works for Paul Ecke. They live up on Saxony."

In the enthusiasm of the moment Fred neglected to ask Dr. Novak the reason for the house call. "I drove over expecting something like measles and arrived just in time to deliver Mrs. Amador's baby," he said. "That battered bag of Dr. Novak's held everything I needed, including lots of newspaper. We used newspapers for home deliveries then, although the dark print rubbed off on the baby. The chemicals in the printing process discouraged germs."

That baby, a boy the Amadors named Charles Frederick, would be the first of 5,778 he delivered locally.

"Fred had a terrific bedside manner. He was fun," remembers Lola Larson whose son, Doran, was born unexpectedly in Fred's office on a day in 1957 when Lola had just gone in for a regular visit.

"He knew my husband would worry," she said. "So when he heard Eric had arrived at the office he propped me up with a beer in one hand, and a sandwich in the other. 'See, Eric—she's doing great,' he said."

Fred, the son of two immigrants--his father was Scottish, his mother English--lived in Del Mar until he was nine, then finished growing up in a 7-bedroom house on the bluffs of Leucadia's Neptune Avenue. "The rent was $35 a month. We'd to scramble to find even that," he said. "It was the Depression. My Dad, who was a true craftsman, was building houses for $1 an hour."

Both he and his younger brother, Jim, wanted, he said, to build houses with their father. But his mother was determined her eldest son would become a doctor.

"What she really wanted was for me to become another Uncle Edward," he said, referring to his mother's brother, Edward Hindle, who, among other things, helped build the Panama Canal, find a cure for Yellow fever, and was Director of the London Zoo. "I remember my Dad saying, 'I'm fed up with hearing how wonderful Edward is!'"

"In 1938 you had to show you'd $10,000 in the bank to get into medical school, so they'd know you were good for the tuition," he said. But while he was putting himself through pre-Med at the University of California by working as a carpenter on Richmond Shipyard's Liberty Ships, (they carried supplies to war-torn Europe), the Army drafted him and paid for the rest of his education at USC.

Fred opened his own general practice in a former department store, Dugals, in Solana Beach's Plaza. It was, he said, "The golden age of medicine." Unimpeded by HMOs he did everything in his office from removing appendixes to repairing hernias, with the receptionist often running the patient home in Fred's station wagon. He had a lot of patients who were officers in the Highway Patrol, which was a little awkward sometimes as his mother, he said, was "the world's worst driver."

"She was lovable and brilliant--one of the first women to go to Stanford when she was sixteen. But her idea of driving was to go until she hit something. The Highway Patrol officer would look at her license and say, 'Dorothy M. Brass. Say, is your son Doctor Brass?' Then they wouldn't want to give her a ticket. 'Oh, but you must,' my mother would insist, and I'd always end up paying them because she could never hold on to money."

Many of Fred's patients were show business stars who came down every summer for the races. One night he got a call from Mexico, from Desi Arnaz's boat captain. Desi had fallen off a verandah when a railing broke.

"He hit the stalk of an old poinsettia and had a swelling about the size of a soccer ball in his side," Fred said.

"I'd recently sold my plane. So I rented a Cessna and flew down to this tiny seaside place, San Warnico, in the middle of the night with no navigational guide," Fred remembers.

When he landed on the main street of the village the mayor came running out of his house yelling, "Senor, you cannot park your plane there!" Eventually they got things sorted out and Fred escorted poor Desi, who'd ruptured an artery near his kidney, back to civilization and Scripps Hospital.

Jimmy Durante was another of Fred's patients who, like Desi, became a close friend.

"When Jimmy was recovering from a stroke I told him I'd know he was recovered when he could play his theme song 'Inka Dinka Doo'," Fred said. "He came over to my house and played it. After he left we noticed he'd left his fedora hat on top of the piano." He really wanted to keep that fedora, Fred said, as a permanent part of the piano. "But Barbara, my wife, insisted we return it to Jimmy."

By the time Fred retired, after thirty-eight years in The Plaza, he'd amassed thirty thousand patient's medical records.

"The Amadors weren't the only parents who named their baby after him" Barbara Brass said. "There are a lot of 50-year-old Freds in the area now."

CHAPTER FOUR

"Green Valley School, Floods, Goats and Mr. Loveless"

Written July 2000

    There's a soothing image you might like to hold in mind the next time you find yourself edging through bumper-to-bumper, horn-honking traffic on El Camino Real. If you're anywhere between Encinitas Boulevard and half a mile north of Olivenhain Road, you'll be in the area the pioneers named Green Valley.
    And that's exactly what it was; green and a valley.
    Not only cows grazed there, but sheep as well. A river meandered near the narrow dirt track that became today's six and eight-lane highway. Twice a year, a truant officer with the Dickensian name of Mr. Loveless visited the one-room schoolhouse.

Green Valley's teachers, all females, came and went at the school, which opened in 1895 and closed in the late '30s. But there was always only one teacher, valiantly juggling eight grades.

"The single ones often had to live in a 10-foot by 16-foot wooden house, with kerosene lanterns and no running water," remembered Marguerite Miller, who started at the school in 1921. "And the strange thing was, I can never remember a teacher getting sick. Or even taking one day off."

At least the teachers didn't have to clean the school. That job was given to one of the "big" boys.

In 1920 the "big" boy was Charlie Lillygreen, all of eleven, who was paid $3 a month. "Although it had gone up to $7 by the time I graduated from 8th grade in 1924," Charlie said.

Because most of the children had chores like feeding the hogs before school the first class began at 9 a.m. Charlie arrived around 7:30 to stoke the wood-burning stove. After that he collected the day's water supply, lugging it in buckets from a well on a farm 200 hundred yards away (owned by Marguerite's parents, Alwin and Frieda Wiegand).

"When I started at the school there were only seven of us, all related," he said. For one year only--Charlie thinks it was 1923--the student population swelled to thirty seven." Three Italian families, who brought herds of sheep with them, moved to the area. But they didn't stay long," he said. "Plus we had several Mexican children and a large Russian family called the Prohoffs whose children came to school in a horse and cart."

Dan Wiegand, Marguerite's younger brother, started school in 1928 when he was five.

"The older boys told me horror stories about what the county nurse was going to do to me when she visited," Dan recalled. They terrified him so much, he said, that when he saw the nurse's car coming he raced home, hurtled into the granary and burrowed under a pile of grain sacks.

Another source of great anxiety at the school--not just for Dan, but for most of the pupils--was Alwin Weigand's large, mean Billy goat. "My Dad had bought him because he hoped he'd keep coyotes away from his sheep," Dan said. "But that goat preferred the schoolhouse yard to being up in the hills. Of all the kids, only my brother, Jim, could control him by grabbing his beard."

There was a grove of trees near the school, Dan said, and someone had nailed a plank between two Cypress trees. The entire school--in the late '20s that meant eight or nine children--ate their lunches up there. The teacher, Miss Gilbert, used to summon them down by blowing a whistle.

One day, Dan said, Miss Gilbert was out in the school yard blowing her whistle, but he and two other boys were trapped in the trees by the goat.

"The teacher whacked at him with a push broom," Dan recalled. "But the goat butted her and poor Miss Gilbert went down in the dust with a cry of 'Ooof!'"

As if mean animals and primitive housing conditions weren't enough, Green Valley teachers had to cope with annual floods. When the rains came the river overflowed and El Camino Real turned into thick mud or, in really bad years, a fast churning stream of swirling brown water.

In the schoolhouse any child needing to go to the bathroom had to slosh around the back to either the boy's or girl's outhouse. "We had to wear high boots every time," Richard Scott remembers. "The school's foundation was raised twice because of the floods."

One year, when the rains were so heavy that the area that's now Mountain Vista Road had washed away to a crater, Richard, aged seven, waited at the school for his father, Lucas Scott, to collect him. (The Scott's farm was just east of where Home Depot is now, and the school was half a mile north of Olivenhain Road).

"I waited and waited," Richard said. "Finally my Uncle Alwin sent his hired man over with a horse. I rode home behind him, clutching the edges of his very wet saddle." He reached home, he said, to find his father was out looking for him. "When Dad got back that evening he was pretty mad with me for not waiting."

In the mid '30s the teacher, Jane Cotton, lived with the Scott family. "That was kind of exciting," Richard said. "In the mornings I walked to school with her. After I'd milked the cows."

Parts of the school's original foundation still lurk below El Camino Real, Richard believes. "The road has been widened so much they'd be somewhere in the middle."

"The second foundation was four feet off the ground. Great for games of hide and seek," Dan Wiegand said. "One lunch time Earl Weller thought he'd discovered a weasel under there and prodded it out with a stick." The weasel was actually a skunk. That afternoon, as the entire school was trying to breath though that worse-than-burnt-rubber skunk smell, a car pulled up outside.

Mr. Loveless had chosen that day for one of his surprise inspections. As far as Dan can remember it was an extremely speedy one.

Charlie Lillygreen, who was quoted in this column, died in the early 1990s. Fortunately I was able to quote him because of a video he made for the San Dieguito Heritage Museum.

CHAPTER FIVE

"Fletcher Cove's Lifeguards Thanked with Cookies, $100 Bills"

Written October 2000

    It's been almost fifty years since the "day of the sting rays". It was warm that summer Sunday, almost windless. The ocean at Solana Beach's Fletcher Cove looked as calm, as unthreatening, as bath water; but twenty nine beachgoers were victims of sting rays.
    "The pain lasts around half an hour and is so bad I've seen grown men cry," explained retired lifeguard captain Jim Lathers. "Some people say it hurts as much as having a baby. The only treatment we had for it was to soak the poison out in warm water."

The man doing the soaking that day, for all twenty-nine victims, happened to be lifeguard captain Bill Rumsey.

"He had their feet in every type of pail, bucket and can," Willis Werner reported in the San Diego Union. One woman had managed to sit on a ray and Rumsey had to borrow a wash tub for her.

Rumsey was the first lifeguard captain hired when the rescue service began at Fletcher Cove, in 1941, as a branch of the Sheriff's Department.

"The county had to do something," Lathers said." About 40 people had drowned the previous year."

The entire start-up budget was $1,200, most of which went for a red panel truck that carried such necessities as a resuscitator and a stretcher. It had oversized tires, for getting through soft sand, and, Lathers said, "Looked like something you'd sell fish from."

Rumsey, who, before he retired in 1960, saved 2,887 people from possible drowning, had nine lifeguards in that first crew. Four of them were "weekends only". Between them they had to cover Imperial Beach, Del Mar, Solana Beach, Swamis at Encinitas and South Carlsbad.

"They were an independent bunch," said Lathers, who began lifeguarding in 1950, and took over as captain at Fletcher Cove in 1965. "In those early days there wasn't too much concern about the sun." Nobody wore any kind of sunblock and, although the county issued tropical pith helmets to lifeguards, he said, they were rarely worn. "We wore whatever we felt like on our heads. Everything from a towel, to a Mexican sombrero."

Love of the job, of the exercise, of life in the fresh air, far outweighed the meager pay, Lathers said. In 1941 a lifeguard's pay was $115 a month, $160 for a captain. Most held second jobs, or were college students. William "Red" Shade, a lifeguard every summer from '41 to '81--Red was 60 when made his last rescue --

was a professional musician. Rumsey, a former teacher, used to moonlight as a bouncer at the Mission Bay Ballroom.

County funds were so sparse, in fact, that Rumsey and lifeguard John Rigon built the station house at Fletcher Cove themselves. The lumber they used was leftover from construction at the Torrey Pines military base, Camp Callan.

"There was no hot water at the station house," Lathers remembered. "Every evening, no matter what the wind was like, Bill Rumsey would grab his lava soap and take a cold shower outside, under a pipe that came out of the wall."

Lifeguards carry "rescue cans" with them when they plunge into the sea, so that a swimmer in trouble can hang on to the can's rope handles. These days, although still called "rescue cans," they're made of lightweight, flexible foam. Back in the '40s they were metal, with pointed ends that looked like the Tin Man's hat in The Wizard of Oz.

"I've been told that if a wave pitched one on to your head it hurt," Paul Dean, the current lifeguard captain at Fletcher Cove, said.

People have varied reactions to being rescued from drowning, Dean said. "Most are appreciative. Children are scared, but men are often really embarrassed." In July '41 Willis Werner reported in the San Diego Union that the first words a rescued business man gasped were "What time is it?" Then he complained it had taken so long to rescue him he'd missed an appointment.

The most grateful rescued swimmer of local record is race horse owner and plane parts manufacturer, Bernard Robinson.

In the racing season of 1941 Robinson was swimming off the beach at Del Mar, when a riptide swept him a quarter of a mile out to sea. Lifeguard Bill Southwell didn't have his rescue can with him that day, so he towed a semiconscious Robinson the entire quarter of a mile, using a cross-chest carry.

When they reached the shallow water actor Pat O'Brian, who was Robinson's neighbor, helped to carry him up the beach to his house.

A few days later Robinson gave the 21-year-old Southwell a check for one thousand dollars, and a black Chevy convertible with red seats.

Nothing like that has happened in the twenty nine years since he became a lifeguard, Dean said."But people have brought us cookies or written a nice card. Once, only once, a grateful guy came in and handed around one hundred dollar bills."

Apart from the addition of a garage, Fletcher Cove's wooden lifeguard station (now known as the Marine Safety Department) looks much as it did when Rumsey and Rigon hammered it up in 1943. On one window ledge a plastic baggie holds two greyish, bone-like objects a few inches long. Their edges are serrated, treacherously sharp.

"They're from the tails of sting rays," Dean explained. The largest number of sting ray victims he can remember taking care of himself in a single day is three, he said.

"The day when there were twenty nine of them must have been really something."

CHAPTER SIX

"Leaving Cardiff-By-The-Sea"

Written March 1998

Some of the Backward Glance columns are personal stories. The "American Gothic" illustration above is my son Craig's version of how he imagined his father and I looked when we moved to Cardiff-By-The-Sea in 1961.

In 1979, when I was writing for a San Diego newspaper, I interviewed a sweet-faced Hispanic woman named Lucy Barrajas Guerrero. Lucy's father, Hilario Barraras, had built a house on Cardiff's Dublin Drive in 1927, when the town was a sea of vegetable fields and flowers, a handful of buildings and very little else. String beans, and Italian squash, and asters covered the hills that are now covered with houses.

"The hills were full of coyotes then," Lucy told me. Owls hooted softly in the dusk and red rattlesnakes twisted silently into their Dublin garden.

"My father caught several of the rattlesnakes. They were deadly poisonous, but we kept them in cages as pets," she said. "The garden was also full of these tiny birds--'Tildeo' birds we called them--that sounded like a baby crying."

I kept thinking of Lucy last week, as we were packing up to leave Cardiff-By-The-Sea after living on Montgomery Avenue for 37 years.

Not that we went far; just from Cardiff to Encinitas. Our large, older home was rather like an aging actress, fraying around the edges, but charming.

Even with the charm and the current insane market, I was surprised by the number of people who wanted to buy it (our realtor, George, got the first query as he was hammering his sign into the middle of the daffodils.) The biggest surprise, though, wasn't the selling part, but how much buying a home has changed since 1961.

In 1961 we didn't even have a contract. A down payment and a handshake was about all it took.

Now, as anyone who has bought a home around here knows, as you wait out the suspense of escrow, whisking between building inspections and termite tenting, every few days someone waves a document in front of you.

"Sign here....and here....and your initials here, please. Oh, and, ha! ha! I guess we missed that little sucker on page 114."

In 1961 we simply took the house "as is."

Not that "as is" turned out to be all that great. Our house was what was known then as a Hunsaker Home. In the early '50s an enterprising builder named Hunsaker dotted the hills of Cardiff with small, square houses, with carports instead of garages. You can still see a few of the originals around, but very few. Most of them have either been torn down, or their owners have, as we did, remodeled them beyond recognition.

Mr. Hunsaker had put them up cheaply and plumbed them with pipes destined to either corrode rapidly or become choked with tree roots, whichever came first.

Free-spirited renters had painted the interior walls of our Hunsaker the kind of pink, purple and green normally seen only in day-glo pens. They throbbed with color, those walls. On our first week-end there my husband, Scotty, leaned against one of them and his hand went straight through the plaster.

A kitchen cabinet fell off another day-glo wall, smashing most of our wedding china. And when I tried to put the baby, Gordon, aged four months, on a patch of grass at the back, a male head appeared over the fence and said, "Wouldn't do that if I were you. See that tree? Castor beans. Poison. Carry the little guy off in no time."

Once those problems were solved, though, Cardiff was a lovely place to live. This was before the days of the lets-build-a-house-as-big-as-the-average-hospital got started. Perched on our hill we could see the whole dazzling sweep of the ocean and the lagoon (it was called a slough in those days). Three bright pink flamingoes were living in the slough--on the lam from the San Diego Zoo perhaps?--and at night the cars coming down 101 formed a twisting ribbon of lights reflected in the water.

We were new immigrants then and I used to write eat-your-heart-out letters to my British relatives, saying things like, "Oh, wow! We actually have a banana tree in our back yard." (For 20 years this tree didn't produce a single banana and when it finally produced a flower it turned out to be a Bird of Paradise plant.)

Last week, the night before we moved, I climbed the hill behind our soon-to-be-former-house and tried to picture Cardiff as it must have looked when Lucy Barajas Guerrero first saw it, as a 4-year-old, in 1918.
They'd come, Lucy and her family, by train, making a long, dangerous journey across a Mexico ravaged by the revolution. She remembered her mother throwing a blanket over her , trying to shield her eyes from the sight of the firing squad victims hanging on poles beside the tracks.
"When we reached Cardiff-By-The-Sea it looked like paradise to us," she said. "The hills were covered in lavender-blue brodiae and the beach was a mass of yellow poppies."
It was paradise with a catch, though. When her father built his house in Cardiff neighbors who objected to having a Mexican family there nailed up their outside toilet during the night. But, eventually, Lucy said, the neighbors became very friendly.
"My mother and I used to walk hand in hand along Edinburg. It was just a sandy track then and our sandals were always full of dust," she said. "But Cardiff was so beautiful."
"So many things vanished as the houses began springing up. The Tildeo birds, the roadrunners and quails, the poppies and the blue wild grass iris in the bushes. But some things....well, some things in Cardiff are much, much better now."

CHAPTER SEVEN

"Amelia's Wedding Gift"

Written February 1999

Whenever I drive past Herb Lux's land, which is on Cardiff's Manchester Avenue beside the gold-domed Greek church, I think about Amelia's wedding present.

Amelia was Herb's mother. She began life in the 1890s, the blonde-haired, blue-eyed youngest daughter of Olivenhain pioneers Adam and Christiana Wiegand.

"It was a tradition among the pioneer families to give land as a wedding present," Herb told me.

So when Amelia married Alexander Lux, whose parents, like the Wiegands, were German pioneers, the young couple's wedding gifts included 200 acres of Cardiff.

Today most people would consider owning 200 acres of Cardiff an occasion for setting off rockets at high noon. "But when my mom and dad came here in 1919, you could have counted the number of families on one hand," Herb said.

Alex and Amelia settled down to life on a lima bean farm. Alex did all the outside work. Amelia did the inside work, milked the cow and managed the 300 or so chickens. By 1926 she was also managing three tow-headed sons.

Jesse and Robert were born in the farmhouse. Herbert, the youngest, arrived unexpectedly one afternoon while Amelia was in Olivenhain visiting her mother. Knowing his Grandmother Wiegand, Herb said, "She probably calmly put down her tea cup and coped."

Before I met Herb I'd always imagined life in Cardiff in the '30s as pretty quiet. But the lives of the Luxs were dotted with lively moments.

There was, for instance, Ed Morgan, their neighbor who loved dynamite. Morgan farmed on the corner of Manchester and El Camino Real, where the sculpture studio is now. "We never knew when Ed was going to set off an explosion," Herb remembers. "His uncle George who lived with him was almost deaf and once when Ed had blasted off ten sticks Uncle George muttered, 'Sounds like there's something on the roof.'"

Dynamite was sold over the counter then at the Encinitas hardware store and every July 4th, before dawn, Ed Morgan would blow up part of his land to celebrate. "Nobody stopped him. People had a lot more freedom then to do whatever they took it into their heads to do," Herb said.

Uncle Roy, Alex Lux's brother, once took it into his head to mail two baby alligators from Florida to the Encinitas Post Office. "They arrived inside Kraft Cheese boxes," Herb remembers. "The one intended as a gift for cousin Norma was last seen escaping in the direction of the La Costa Lagoon, but the one Uncle

Roy sent to my brother Bob lived on our farm for years, growing bigger, and meaner, and hissing at visitors."

The world of Cardiff in the '30s was one where the clothes on almost everyone's back came from Montgomery Ward or Sears Roebuck Catalogs: where men drove not only their tractors but their Model T cars straight across the fields because there were no roads. A world where bottles of home-brewed beer sometimes exploded, splashing flowered wallpaper, and wives bought tins of tea, carbolic soap and cod liver oil pills from the traveling Raleigh Man.

There were, too, the big dramas.

A plane crashed in the lima bean fields. A ship carrying kegs of whiskey sank off Moonlight Beach. One night a man named Red Calderwood, a hired man on the Lux's farm, came close to burning the place to the ground.

"Dad's pride and joy, a shiny blue Willis-Knight car, was kept in the machine shed with the tractor," Herb said. "One night, when dad was away from home, Calderwood drove the tractor in from the fields and filled it with gasoline." The engine, unfortunately, was still hot. Flames exploded, shooting up the shed's walls.

"Ed Morgan, the neighbor who loved dynamite, saw the red glow in the sky and rushed over to help," Herb said. "He jumped in the Willis-Knight, but couldn't figure out how to start it, so he pushed it from the shed. We were all outside, with mom yelling, 'Kids, stay back!' Bob's hair got a little singed, but the house wasn't damaged at all."

Sunday Feasts were a very big part of the '30s. Aunt Lizzie, Amelia's sister Elizabeth, was married to Lucas Scott whose three hundred and fifty acres stretched across the Green Valley area. The sisters alternated cooking the Sunday Feasts.

"Always eaten after church, with almost everything home-grown," said Herb, who still remembers the pot roasts with rich gravy, the thick cream poured over pies lush with pears, apricots and peaches.

Amelia's specialty was noodles, which she used to drape over the backs of the farmhouse chairs to dry.

These days Herb still lives where he grew up, but on not quite two acres. If you're driving past it's easy to imagine the farm on a Saturday night in the '30s. In the yellow light of oil lamps Alex turns the pages of the Southern California Rancher , as his sons wrestle on the slippery linoleum floor.

And Amelia? Amelia is heating her curling iron in the chimney of a lamp, because tomorrow there'll be church and the Sunday Feast.

CHAPTER EIGHT

"Christiana, Portrait of a Pioneer"

Written March 1998

Christiana appeared in the previous chapter. She was Amelia Lux's mother.

It was the photograph that drew me into Christiana's story. Taken in 1895, on a homestead in Aliso Canyon (now Rancho Santa Fe), it showed a fair-haired woman standing in a clod-filled, dusty field with her husband and her four, small tow-headed children. She looked so neat, so tidy. Her white apron, rising above the bump of a fifth child, had the brightness of a modern Tide commercial. How, living in a house without water, did she manage it?

"Every day she'd put a yoke with two buckets over her shoulders and struggled back and forth, to and from, the creek," her granddaughter, Mary Ann Wood, told me. "She made her own soap, stirring fat and lye in a big pot over the fire. When it hardened it was rock solid and the color of mozzarella cheese, but it worked just fine."

Lack of water was a constant problem. "She had a way of feeding cattle in the dry years that probably came from the Indians in this area. Very early, before the wind came up, she'd fill her apron with sticks from dried bushes. Then, surrounded by hungry cattle watching with anxious eyes, she'd pile sticks around several cactus and set them on fire. Once the thorns burnt off, the cattle could eat them."

I was sitting at Mary Ann's kitchen table as she explained all this. The brown-green stretch of Olivenhain that showed beyond her kitchen windows was the same land her grandparents, Adam and Christiana Wiegand, moved to in 1903, eight years after that "dusty field" photograph was taken. Today the land still qualifies as back country, but busy Manchester Avenue skirts Mary Ann's driveway and, within half a mile, curves past the gold dome of the Greek church, and MiraCosta's Cardiff campus.

Adam Wiegand was Christiana's second husband. Her story has all the drama of a T.V. mini-series. Born in Heilbron, Germany, she emigrated to Chicago as a young girl. Adam, also a German immigrant, a good-natured fellow with reddish blond hair and a droopy mustache, noticed the rosy-cheeked Christiana in the rooming house where he lodged. Probably, based on his later actions, he more than noticed her, but he couldn't do anything about his feelings because she was already married to a man named Schmidt, a sausage-maker.

"A family legend is that grandmother's first husband was killed in a barroom fight," Mary Ann said. "But that's not quite what happened. My second cousin, Beverly, managed to track down an old newspaper account from 1886.

Schmidt was in favor of meat workers joining a union and happened to be at a meeting about this held in a bar. Tempers flared and someone struck the poor man on the side of the head with a mallet."

Christiana was left with $2,000 life insurance and, possibly, a baby on the way. No one's really sure about the baby because at that point Adam, who'd been farming in Olivenhain, returned to Chicago to collect a young lady he intended to marry. He changed his mind when he discovered Christiana was newly widowed and married her so quickly, the family have never been certain who fathered the first Wiegand baby born in this area.

There were five of them eventually. Alwin, Elizabeth, Herman, Amelia and Fritz. (Fritz was the "bump" in the 1895 photograph.) All were delivered on the homestead by midwife Maria Osuna.

Her first years as a farmer's wife couldn't have been easy ones for Christiana. She was deeply religious and the nearest church was in Escondido, a four or five hour wagon ride over bumpy roads. The work on the farm was never-ending: she milked, planted, scrubbed, pickled, sewed and baked. (When he was 102, her son Herman, Mary Ann's father, could still recall the way the smell of his mother's bread baking drifted across the homestead from her outdoor "beehive" oven). She longed for fruit trees and tried to grow them, lugging water to her trees in buckets. She cried when they died.

She gardened all her life and grew enormous cabbages that she turned into sauerkraut to keep her family healthy in winter, in the days before vitamin pills and refrigerators. (Her original sauerkraut-cutter can be seen in the San Dieguito Heritage Museum on Vulcan Avenue, in Encinitas).

"When grandfather died in 1921, she moved into that house over there," Mary Ann said, pointing through her kitchen window to where a red roof glimmered through the trees. "She lived there for twenty-nine years, speaking German, although she could speak English. When I was small I'd walk up the hill to visit her and in the stillness of the morning I'd hear her singing German hymns."

Christiana lived to be ninety four. She died in the Spring of 1950; exactly ten years before water was piped into Olivenhain.

CHAPTER NINE

"Eden Gardens' Pool-Playing Twins "

Written July 2001

"I didn't know what I was getting into," Bobby Rincon said, recalling a suspense-filled afternoon about thirty-five years ago at Del Mar's Firepit restaurant (now The Poseidon). It was an afternoon when he played seven straight games of pool for $7,000 a game.

Not that Bobby wasn't used to playing pool. His home, while he was growing up, was The Blue Bird restaurant in Eden Gardens. His father Guillermo Rincon--known as G.R.--had opened The Blue Bird in 1937 as a pool hall and beer and wine bar. The following year his wife Ramona gave birth to identical twin boys, Bobby and Raymond.

By the time they were seven, Bobby said, they were working in the pool hall, "earning five cents a game as rack boys."

By fifteen Bobby was already gaining a reputation as a player it was hard to beat. Of the $7,000 a game match at The Firepit he remembers his opponent simply as The Man From La Jolla.

"A friend called me and said, 'Come on down. This guy's beating everyone!'" remembers Bobby, whose nickname was E.G. (Eden Gardens) Fats, after pool-playing legend Minnesota Fats. "When I got there the room was packed, full of Del Mar businessmen and just about every friend I had, including Victor Mature."

Bobby didn't have much money on him. It would be his friends' money he'd be playing with.

The Man From La Jolla's smile was almost a sneer.

"So you're the Mexican kid they brought over to beat me," he said.

They played in absolute silence, broken only by the click of the balls, the occasional nervous cough from the watchers. After seven games The Man From La Jolla had lost $49,000.

"I put out my hand and said, 'This is the Mexican kid who beat you,'" Bobby remembers. "But he turned away, snapped his pool cue in half, and walked out."

Bobby's father, G.R., born in 1900, came from the Mexican state of Michchoacan in his 20s, and opened Carlsbad's first pool hall in the barrio. In those days alcohol was illegal in the United States.

"My father and his friend Juan Salvador Villasenor would walk across the border from Mexico wearing long, flapping coats with about 12 pockets," Bobby said. "There'd be a bottle hidden in every pocket."

The Blue Bird, he said, evolved into a restaurant because of a window in the wall between the family's kitchen and the pool hall. "My mother was a wonderful cook. When customers got hungry they'd lean into our kitchen and say, 'Hey, Ramona, can you make me something?'"

Behind the restaurant G.R.'s pet coyote roamed on a long rope tied to a tree.

"My Dad always loved coyotes. That pet one would eat from his hand, play with him, but when he'd take customers out to see it they could never get near," Bobby remembers.

G.R. died in 1950, leaving Ramona with four sons, one daughter and The Blue Bird.

"She also had five children she'd adopted when relatives died," Bobby said.

At the funeral G.R.'s old friend Juan Salvador Villasenor, who was Bobby and Raymond's godfather, offered to adopt the 12-year-old twins. "My mother refused," Bobby said. "He was a rich man. I used to tease her that she should have said 'Yes!'"

By their early teens the twins were playing pool against the customers for $5 a game.

As no one could tell them apart sometimes they switched in midgame. "We're mirror twins. Raymond is is left-handed, I'm right," Bobby explained. "If a left-handed shot was called for--one a right-handed player would have to make holding the cue behind his back--I'd excuse myself to go to the bathroom."

"Raymond would walk out, make the shot, and we'd switch back."

As soon as he turned twenty-one Bobby took over managing The Blue Bird's bar. All Ramona's children worked in The Blue Bird, he said, except for Raymond. At eighteen Raymond married Teresa Gonzales, whose parents, Tony and Catalina, owned Tony's Jacal just up the street. "Raymond went to work at Tony's, and he's been there forty five years," Bobby said.

The twins got married on the same day in 1957, but four hours apart Bobby's bride, Sally, cooked and waitressed at The Blue Bird for the next thirty-eight years. Her friendliness, Bobby said, helped build up the business. "I can remember Joe Hernandez, the announcer at the race track, coming in year after year. He'd call out to Sally, to make him a special fish dish that he liked and she would always make it for him." Momma Ramona--as most of the regular customers affectionately called her--cooked at The Blue Bird until her eighties. Six months ago, at ninety, she sold the building. Bobby has heard it's going to be pulled down but hasn't, he says, seen it lately. "I don't want to. To many memories there."

But the Eden Gardens house where he was born and spent the first two years of his life is still there.

Sam Lunde, who owns Solana Beach's Tidewater Tavern, where Bobby now runs the bar from Wednesdays to Saturdays, remembers asking him where he was born.

"Most people will tell you something like 'San Diego' or 'Chicago'," Sam said. "But Bobby told me, 'The little house across the street from The Blue Bird.'"

CHAPTER TEN

"VG Donuts"

Written October 1999

If you didn't live in Cardiff thirty years ago it may sound like an extreme statement to say that VG Donuts was our small town's heart. It was, though.

"This used to be the community center--everyone would meet here and discuss community business," said Andrew Beckers, who, with his wife, Frances, has been a regular customer since 1970.

It was smaller in those days, with a single long counter from which, sitting wreathed in smells of warm baking, of caramel and vanilla, you could watch owner Jim Mettee braiding dough or dipping fresh donuts into liquid chocolate.

At that counter, almost daily, you'd see Joe-the-poet scribbling endlessly into a notebook the size of a cigarette package. Charlie-who-loved-women was another regular. (It didn't matter what you looked like, if you were female Charlie would lie valiantly and exclaim, "You're looking gorgeous today!"). One of the evening regulars was a math professor from UCSD who planned all his lessons at the counter.

"And then there was the man who changed seats," remembers Maureen Mettee. "He'd move gradually up the counter, seat by seat, getting a fresh cup of coffee each move."

In all the times I visited VGs--two hundred, maybe?--I can't remember seeing a kid really misbehave there. Jim Mettee, tall and pale in a white shirt, crisp white pants that somehow, stayed immaculate underneath his apron, set the tone of the place. He never raised his voice, but he didn't have to. Kids loved Jim. His patience even extended to my son, Craig, who was about three when I began taking him to VGs. Craig used to charm quarters from the regulars and play the same juke box song over and over--something about riding through the desert on a horse with no name--and then he'd dance on the shiny linoleum while I sat there murmuring,"I do hope he's not bothering anyone?"

VGs was called V 'n Gs when Jim and Betty Mettee bought it in 1969. "The V and G were the first letters of the names of a previous owner's daughters, " Betty said. "We just dropped the 'n'."

That first year they had a contract to supply doughnuts to the Del Mar Race Track. Jim spent most of the night making them. Maureen, the eldest of their six children, would also go in at night to pack the doughnuts and Betty, with her 14-year-old son Joe, delivered them to the track at 4 a.m. and 6 a.m.

"One night my dad finished the doughnuts and put them out in the alley, on high metal racks, to cool, " Maureen remembers. "A garbage truck came through and knocked the lot flying. Poor Dad had to start all over again."

With the exception of Jim Junior, all the Mettee's children--Maureen, Anne, Joe, John and Jerry--worked at VGs. "I used to worry they spent too much time working," Betty said. "But one day in JC Penny's I was watching a clerk having trouble making change from a $100 bill and my youngest, Jerry, who was seven, figured it out easily. That made me feel better." (Recently, Betty said, she learned her kids used to stand on VGs roof and have dough-throwing fights with the Corder's kids, who were on the roof of their parents' Besta-Wan Pizza House.)

"VGs was Nirvana for kids," my eldest son, Gordy, said. He and his buddy Myron Stam used to stop in on their way home from Cardiff Elementary school whenever Myron's big sister, Debbie, was working. "Debbie would give us the unsalable floor doughnuts," Gordy remembers. "The ones that had fallen on the floor."

In those days VGs stayed open twenty four hours. Throughout the night the police came in for their coffee breaks. But when the police weren't there, Betty said, Jim often helped someone in trouble who'd come in after seeing the shop's light blooming in the darkened shopping center. Nights at VGs were quite different from days. Sometimes some of the customers were scary.

Maureen remembers being alone at 5 a.m. when a man walked in. "I was reaching into the glass doughnut case," she said. "And when I looked up there was another man next to him holding a gun to his head. The FBI were picking him up!"

1980 was a year of change. "The lease of the Laundromat next-door was up," Betty said. VGs expanded into it and became VG Donuts and Bakery. Shortly afterwards Jim retired and his son Joe, at twenty-four, a ten-year veteran of the business, took over.

Today VGs is still a family business. Maureen and John Mettee work there part-time. Joe, very much his father's son, has kept the tradition of making donuts so delicious that, once tasted, they are never forgotten. Another tradition of his father's that he's kept is the one of hiring friendly help. There's always a lot of laughter bouncing around that place.

The counter, though, that former local political hotbed, that formica stretch where Joe-the-poet once scribbled and Charlie-who-loved-women flirted, has never been quite the same since the expansion.

As Gordy remarked when I told him I was writing about VGs, "It was almost like the people at that counter were the local royalty of gossip--and when VGs expanded the court disbanded."

CHAPTER ELEVEN

"Aladdin's Cave--The Wilkens Wonderful Store"

Written May 1999

The Wilkens brothers were very young, George was four and Bob only two, the day in 1925 when their parents, Gustave (Duke) and Florence led them down a dusty trail in Solana beach.

"We were going to a beach picnic with Dad's friend, Hershell Larrick Sr. and his family," George Wilkens remembers. Larrick, who had opened the Solana Lumber and Builders Supply in 1922 (he also owned lumber yards in Del Mar and Encinitas), had to get down the trail on a crutch.

"He'd lost a leg in San Diego when he slipped and fell under a street car," George explained. "Our dad had also fallen under one, but he'd only lost part of a toe so felt, by comparison, it was hardly worth mentioning. "

The picnic came to a dramatic end when Larrick was bitten on his remaining foot by a sting ray. Both boys have a hazy memory of their father kneeling on the sand and sucking out the poison from his friend's foot.

"That same year," Bob said, "Mr. Larrick persuaded Dad to move from Escondido to Solana Beach to manage the lumber yard."

In 1933 Duke Wilkens, with Larrick's blessing, bought out the lumber yard's entire stock of gardening supplies. He opened G.G. Wilkens Ranch & Garden Supplies where the corner of Cedros Avenue meets Lomas Santa Fe. It flourished there for the next fifty three years.

If you were ever a customer during those years you'll remember the "Aladdin's Cave" feel of the place, the stairs in unexpected places (it was built into the side of the hill), the massive inventory, the aisles that grew progressively narrower the further back you went.

"Dad, with Mom helping at first, began in one little building," George said. "But it kept growing, with a hodgepodge of add-ons." In 1937, when the race track was built on the site of Del Mar's golf course, Duke bought the golf course club house and added that on, too.

Running the business involved a lot of strenuous lifting and hauling. The local ranchers bought their supplies in bags weighing 100 lbs. "The Japanese truck farmers, who were here before World War II, would come in and buy ten tons of fertilizer," George remembers. By the time the brothers were in their early teens they were tossing 150 lb. hay bales onto the delivery trucks. By fourteen they were driving the trucks.

"Not just a pickup. Big trucks, hauling five, six tons," Bob said. "Dad offered free delivery with every purchase."

Some of the customers to whom they delivered were celebrities, including opera singer Madame Galicuchi, Robert Young, Harry James and Bing Crosby. Bob made many deliveries to Rancho Zoro, in Rancho Santa Fe, where Douglas Fairbanks, Sr. had a thousand acres of orange groves.

"The oil they used on Rancho Zoro to mix the insect repellent came in fifty gallon drums," Bob remembers. "And usually I had to unload about thirty of them each trip." But there were, he says, compensations.

"San Dieguito Chamber of Commerce threw great annual parties on Rancho Zoro and Fairbanks always showed his latest movie on a screen set up by the lake."

The brothers did take time off for college and serving in World War II. In the '50s, their father ran the store eighty percent of the time, while Bob and George specialized in sprinkler systems, stone walls and patios.

"We got the stone from Calaveras Quarry in Carlsbad, breaking it up with a 16 lb. sledgehammer," George recalled. "Like prisoners on a chain gang!"

Duke Wilkens died in 1966 . "Mom came back to work in the office then because she wanted to keep busy," George said. "She always had an outgoing personality and the customers loved her. She worked there until she was eighty nine."

Saturdays in the store were, Bob said, "A madhouse. At one time we counted a hundred people milling about. Our little business secret was that you have to have something no one else has. "

The Wilkens had a lot of "somethings" no one else had, which worked well until the annual inventory-taking, which both describe as "No fun at all."

"It was the kind of business where many customers became good friends," Bob said. "Of course we had occasional problems with them. I remember one kid who kept wandering in and helping himself to the free doughnuts we always served, with coffee, on Saturdays. Finally, I took him aside and told him, 'You know, those doughnuts are for the paying customers.' The next Saturday he bought a ten-cent package of seeds and gave me a big smile. Later in the day he brought the seeds back for a refund!"

The Wilkens brothers retired in 1986. The "Aladdin's Cave" buildings have been torn down; replaced by Solana Plaza. But when George and Bob walk along Cedros it's all still here in memories--the trucks they loaded with 150 lb. bales of hay, the hectic Saturdays, the struggle of figuring out inventory, the customers who were good friends and even the smile on the face of the kid with the ten-cent packet of seeds.

CHAPTER TWELVE

"Tak Sugimoto--Going Home to Encinitas "

Written May 2000

"When Takedo Sugimoto collected his graduation diploma at San Dieguito High School our entire class of '45 broke into cheers," Ida Lou Coley remembers. They were cheering, she said, because they'd all gone through school with Tak--

some of them from kindergarten--but three years earlier he'd been taken away to an internment camp.

Before his family were imprisoned, though, Tak found Encinitas a wonderful place in which to grow up.

"Everyone knew everyone and kids roamed freely," he said of the days when his parents' farmhouse sat on the spot that's now the YMCA on Saxony Road.

Fields of strawberries, blackberries, celery, cucumber and squash surrounded his home. Tak and his friends swam in Bark Canyon's swimming holes behind La Costa, and hunted the red rattlesnakes that once infested the area now Skyloft Homes, above Batiquitos lagoon. They followed the tar trucks, occasionally scooping up and chewing lumps of warm black tar when, in 1936, the roads were black-topped.

"The roads were only dirt before then," he said. "There was nothing but open land between our farm and downtown Encinitas. A 22-rifle bullet will travel a mile and my friends and I used to stand on the hill and shoot at a telephone pole a mile away. It was so quiet then, we'd know we'd hit it if we heard a 'ping'."

Sajiro and Yoshire Sugimoto moved to Encinitas, with son Kozo, four, daughter Fusaye, two, and baby daughter, Kiyo, in 1925. That was two years before Tak was born. In 1925 there was only one other Japanese family in town, the Itos.

"My father had emigrated to San Francisco when he was twenty two, arriving just in time to lose his papers in the 1906 earthquake," Tak said. "He worked as a fisherman in San Diego and saved his money until he could afford a boat. Then he sent home to Japan for a 'picture bride'."

Soft-spoken Yoshire, the bride Sajiro chose from her picture, had been raised in a time when Japanese women walked behind their husbands. "My mother's philosophy was one of acceptance, of 'what happens, happens,'" Tak said.

The Sugimotos couldn't own land in Encinitas because of the Oriental Exclusion Act (since repealed) so they leased sixty acres. Sajiro looked forward to the day when his eldest son, Kozo, turned twenty-one. As an American-born citizen he'd be able to buy land.

"But by the time Kozo turned twenty-one, in the Spring of '42, he was in an internment camp," Tak said.

Within a week of America going to war with Japan, in December 1941, Japanese families in California were restricted to travel no further than seven miles from home, Tak remembers. "We were also ordered to take all guns, cameras and radios to the police station on San Diego's Front Street. And that was thirty miles away." They even had to destroy their photo albums, he said, in case something useful to a spy might be lurking in a photograph's background.

By April 1942 the Sugimoto family, including Fusaye's husband and baby, were all living in one room on Block 43 of Poston Camp 1 in the Arizona desert.

"Except for my father who was ill with TB. He was shipped to a hospital camp," said Tak, who never saw his father again. "Then, when we'd been at the camp a few months, Kozo was drafted into the American army."

In spite of the armed guards, the scorpions, a climate that swung from scorching to freezing and a wailing wind that rattled the tar paper walls, the camp of about ten thousand people had its bright spots, including schools.

"The principle of the high school, Arthur Main, was from Encinitas," Tak said. "He'd been the first principal at San Dieguito High. I found having him there really comforting."

Another amazingly bright spot he said was the beauty of the art the internees created. "Many, particularly the Issea, the "first generation", had worked seven days a week most of their lives. They hadn't had time before to create artistically. I saw fish ponds, charcoal drawings, intricately carved wooden lamps that were truly beautiful."

Sajiro Sugimoto, Tak's father, died in 1944. He was sixty years old. Civilian bodies couldn't be shipped in wartime, so all Yoshire received was a cardboard box holding her husband's ashes.

A few months later, in December 1944, the internees were told they could go home if they wished.

"Many stayed because they'd no place to go," remembers Tak, who had managed to get special clearance to leave the camp early. He knew exactly where he wanted to go: to Encinitas, to graduate high school with his friends.

"It was my goal. I was the first Japanese to return to the North County," he said. "It was January 1945. There were farm workers living in our old home, which was no longer our home. The things we'd put in storage had disappeared. My family's sole possession was a truck that Paul Ecke, Sr. had saved for us."

Paul Ecke, Sr. had managed to save things for several Japanese families who'd been interned, Tak remembers." I've always thought that was courageous of him because he was German and there were, of course, some strong anti-German feelings around then."

At first Tak felt apprehensive about coming back. "But not one single person in Encinitas was anything but welcoming," he said.

In other parts of the county it was a different story. One day a teacher at San Dieguito High School, E.K. Dobbins, took Tak with him on a trip to San Diego. As he walked down streets he'd once walked with his father, Tak felt, he said, as if he had a big spotlight on his face and that everyone was looking at him. Store windows bristled with signs saying "No Japanese!" and "We don't serve Japanese!"

"And the store owners who were Japanese had signs saying things like, "We're not Japanese, we're Chinese!" he said.

E.K. Dobbins, who taught business courses at San Dieguito, offered the 17-year-old Tak a home while he finished high school.

"Mr. Dobbins lived in Vista," Tak said." Highway 78 didn't exist then, and we used to zoom to school along Rancho Santa Fe Road in his rattling Studebaker. Gasoline was rationed, and precious, so if he got up a good head of speed on the hills he could practically coast down them."

"Mr. Dobbins and his wife were devout Christians. When someone threatened, in an anonymous letter, to burn down their house if I stayed there, I was really worried about it. They had been so kind to me. But they calmly ignored the threat," Tak said.

Today, fifty five years after his classmates gave him that rousing cheer, Tak is a pharmacist at La Costa Pharmacy, which he owns. He and his wife Ruth, (who was also in Camp Poston 1), have five grown children.

"I often wish my children could see how beautiful this area was when I was growing up here," he said.

CHAPTER THIRTEEN

"Sid Shaw and the Riffraff Boys"

Written November 1999

    If you happen to be in Del Mar's Brigantine restaurant on a Tuesday and notice three seventy-something gentlemen roaring with laughter, you're probably seeing Sid Shaw and his friends, Fred Brass and Bob Grice. Friends since they met at San Dieguito High in the 1930s, Sid, Fred and Bob have met for lunch almost every week since the '50s.
    Sixty years ago, though, Sid's mother thought Fred and Bob were a bad influence on him. "She called them 'riffraff boys'," Sid remembers. "Because we went to a lot of parties. We drove fast cars."

Of the three friends only Sid wasn't born in Encinitas, but in Los Angeles. At the age of ten he began playing his trumpet in the band of golden-haired evangelist Aimee Semple McPherson.

"My trumpet teacher was in her band and asked if I could sit in, " Sid said. "We played in the orchestra pit of her Angelus Temple from 6 p.m to 7 p.m. as the crowds filed inside. Then we'd accompany her as she sang. She had a wonderful, throaty voice, like a New Orleans jazz singer, and she played the piano standing up."

Friday nights were the nights when Aimee Semple McPherson performed "miracle healings."

"People would throw their crutches away or rise from their wheelchairs," Sid remembers. "There were rumors they were all actors and actresses. I wouldn't know, but I do remember her personality was so electric that if she came into a room when your back was turned you'd know she was there."

Sid's mother Emma, an English nurse, had emigrated to America by herself while she was still in her teens. "She was twenty six years younger than my father, John Shaw," Sid said.

"As a small boy in 1874, my father had survived an Indian wagon train massacre. "He was sixty-five when I was born and he died when I was eight."

So when his mother moved to Encinitas in 1935, it was with her second husband, retired arson investigator George McClure.

"We lived in a house on Coast Highway 101 that's now The Java Hut coffee house opposite Hansen's," Sid said. "Mom loved surf fishing. Whenever the tide was in, even if it was 1 a.m., she'd be clattering down the stairs by Swamis in her fishing hat and clutching her rod."

On Sid's first day at San Dieguito High he was fifteen and, he said, "extremely skinny. Coming towards me I saw this kid with round glasses and wide suspenders holding up his pants. It was Bob Grice. I thought, wow, that guy's as skinny as I am!"

Sid played his trumpet in a local band, "The Swingsters", but there were few steady jobs in Encinitas for high school graduates of 1938. Briefly, he took over his older brother John's job as a mortician's helper. "I got a dollar a trip from Jim Starbuck for helping him transport bodies," he said. "On my first night we got a call from a Leucadia motel to collect a married couple who'd been asphyxiated by an old-fashioned gas heater. The motel was called 'The Journey's End'."

"I think you should get a job in Los Angeles," Sid remembers his mother urging him. "She was so determined to separate me from my riffraff friends, she even filled my Model A with gas before she waved me off."

Whenever he could Sid returned to North County. He returned as a naval cadet learning to fly, as a commander pilot and in 1944 with his bride LaVerne. Near the end of World War II he flew blimps out of Del Mar's blimp base.

"I wanted to stay after the war," he said," But, again, there weren't many jobs." LaVerne's grandparents in Yuma, Arizona suggested he take over their dry cleaning plant.

"There was no air-conditioning in the plant, only ceiling fans. In July the temperature at midnight reached 117 degrees. At noon it reached 128," he said. "After eight months working there I'd lost so much weight I needed wider suspenders than Bob's!"

In October 1946, while visiting a school friend, Earl Payne, Sid discovered Earl's mother wanted to sell her Encinitas dry cleaning business named "Payne My Cleaners". It was four blocks north of Swamis, between F and G Streets, an area blessed with ocean breezes. Within a month Sid with another friend, Bob Anderson, as partner, had signed the papers and renamed it "Surf Cleaners". Built in 1926, the building--which has a long oak counter with a brass foot-rail like a bar in a Western movie--has now been a dry-cleaners for 73 years.

These days Sid owns almost the whole strip of commercial buildings between F and G , from the car wash to the Hydro-Scape. And the former riffraff boys? Well, they turned out to be remarkably respectable. Bob Grice became an accountant and founded the Encinitas firm of Grice, Lund and Tarkington. Fred Brass became a physician based in Solana Beach Plaza.

"When he first went into practice my mother didn't use Fred as her physician because she still thought of him as a boy," Sid remembers. "In her later years she developed diabetes. One day I went to see her and found her sitting with one foot in the oven to get her circulation going."

Sid called Fred, who rushed over and sent her straight to the hospital. "I think that saved her life," Sid said. "She became one of his favorite patients."

CHAPTER FOURTEEN

"The Kickapoos' Giant Kite"

Written December 2000

    This column comes with a cast of characters. The following names are of the fathers and sons who made up the Encinitas YMCA's Kickapoo Indian Guides Tribe in 1964-65.

Father	Son
Eric Larson	Doran Larson
Paul Ecke Jr.	Paul Ecke, 3rd.
Ed Cory	Scott Cory
John Strozyk	David & Kenny Strozyk
George Hone	Rick & David Hone
Rollie Ayers	Bob Ayers

It was a windy February afternoon in 1964 when the Kickapoo Indian Guides first tested their 70 lb. giant kite. They took it up to the bluffs of Leucadia where the Sea Bluff condominiums are now.

"The wind is usually in the west in the afternoons," Eric Larson said. "So we roped the kite behind my Nash Rambler and I took off fast, driving west."

The box-shaped kite, named "The Spirit of Kitty Hawk," was twenty-three feet long and sixteen feet wide, he said. "I'd no idea what was going to happen. I just hoped it would be airborne before I went over the bluffs."

But the kite, he said, "Soared like a bird."

The Kickapoo boys--average age seven--were leaping around the bluffs, waving their arms, cheering wildly. The fathers were cheering, too, Eric said. The fact that all 70 lbs. of it could fly meant they had a shot at winning the "biggest kite" category in the North Coast YMCA's Indian Guide's Kite Day.

The original idea for the kite was thought up by Eric, an air traffic controller and his friend George Hone, an aeronautical engineer.

"But this was definitely a group project, " Eric said. "We needed a big area to work in so we built it on the Ecke Poinsettia Ranch in one of Paul Jr.'s warehouses."

The frame, he said, was bamboo, cut down on the Ecke Ranch. "The bamboo was fastened together with quarter-inch carriage bolts, and the frame covered in greenhouse plastic, also from Ecke's."

Building the kite took them two weeks. "We found we could dismantle it, slip out the poles and roll up the plastic in half an hour," Eric said. "But it took six times as long to get it back together again."

On the day of the contest, held in the parking lot of the Del Mar Fairgrounds, it was a sunny March Saturday. Dozens of kites--entries in "The Most Beautiful" or "The Most Unique" or "The Highest Flying"--filled the air with bright splashes of color. All eight of the Kickapoo boys were electric with excitement, Eric remembers, as they watched their kite being roped to the back of his Rambler. Of the half dozen "biggest kite" entries theirs was far and away the most enormous.

"The YMCA's rule was that you had 10 minutes to get your kite airborne before being disqualified," Eric said. In a strong wind there was really no limit to how high it might fly, he explained. "But we were limited by Federal Aviation Regulations that said we couldn't fly it, without special permission, above one hundred and fifty feet from the ground."

Which turned out not to be a problem because during the judging the Kickapoos' giant kite wouldn't leave the ground at all. "There simply wasn't a strong enough wind," Eric said.

The 1964 trophy for the biggest kite that actually flew went to the Diegueño tribe from Carlsbad's YMCA.

Just as the disappointed Kickapoos were getting ready to take their kite apart, a strong wind skirled through the fairgrounds. Whooshing and rattling, its greenhouse plastic making a noise like a hundred hands clapping, "The Spirit of Kitty Hawk" rose sixty feet into the sky over Del Mar.

"Too late. All we could do was store it away in Paul Ecke, Jr.'s warehouse until the next year," Eric said.

On the day of the 1965 contest it was extremely windy.

"The kite took off right away," Eric said. He was so excited, he remembers, that he leapt from the Rambler to watch. "I was standing there craning my neck upwards when I realized people were yelling at me," he said. In his excitement he'd forgotten to set the Rambler's brake. The giant kite was towing the car across the fairground parking lot.

"With all the fathers and kids racing after it, grabbing for the rope," Eric said.

"The Spirit of Kitty Hawk's" story had a very happy ending. Every kid in the Kickapoo tribe got a trophy that day, handed out by the Mayor of Del Mar, Vic Koss.

"These days the YMCA's Indian Guides can be mothers and sons. Or fathers and daughters. Any combination," Eric said.

But as far as he knows no one else in this area has ever built another 70 lb. kite.

CHAPTER FIFTEEN

"The Colorful Jobs of Ernie Bertoncini"

Written July 1999

    Back in the 1920s, when Del Mar was a small, seaside town without a dentist, Albino Bertoncini developed an agonizing toothache.
    He and his wife, Ruth, and the three youngest of their six children, Esther, Robert and Ernie, climbed into their 1924 Maxwell (a car with wooden-spoked wheels) and headed for a dentist in San Diego.
    "The dentist gave Dad laughing gas and pulled out the tooth," Ernie Bertoncini remembers. "On the way home we discovered it was the wrong tooth, so we had to turn around and go back."

Perhaps you're wondering why so many Bertoncinis went along on father's dental visit? "Kids, then, thought riding in a car was an adventure," Ernie remembers. "We'd go anywhere."

Ernie was born at 220 10th Street in 1919. The house in which his sister Esther lived for sixty years is one of Del Mar's historical homes. It was originally built in 1885 for Del Mar's founder, Jacob Taylor.

"My parents were warm, generous people," Ernie said. "But in those days parents didn't give kids allowances. If you wanted to have any money you found a job."

The first one he found, at eleven, was as a locker boy at Del Mar's Olympic-sized swimming pool. Locals called it "The Plunge".

"They hired young kids because the job required going into both men's and women's locker rooms," Ernie explained. Swimmers rented a towel and an itchy woolen bathing suit with a modest skirt above shorts for both sexes and a big red 'D' on the chest. Famous people staying at the Hotel Del Mar often used the pool, including English channel-swimmer Florence Chadwick.

"Most people tipped a nickel. The biggest tip I ever got was from movie actress Zasu Pitts," Ernie said. Zasu, who'd shot to fame in 1924's "Greed" (now on video), once gave him a quarter for carrying her umbrella and backrest down to the beach.

By twelve Ernie had a before-school job, too. A dairy farmer named Hillman drove him and classmate Virginia Dunham around delivering milk. It came in thick glass bottles with ivory-colored cream that rose to the top.

"Virginia would go to one side of a street, I'd go to the other," Ernie said. "But when we reached the house of Herman Kockritz, who owned the Kockritz Building on 15th Street, Mr. Hillman always said, 'I'll take this one!' He and Mr. Kockritz would enjoy a couple of drinks together, while Virginia and I waited outside."

As wages Ernie received 2 quarts of milk, half a pint of coffee cream and whipping cream if his mother needed some.

As he moved into his teens he had a variety of Del Mar jobs. He was a ball boy on the hotel tennis courts (the uniform included a leather bow tie) and picked up paper at the race track. By seventeen he was working in the Richfield station at 101 and 14th, which supported his dates with girls in the bright yellow Ford Model A his sister had helped him to buy.

The best-paid job Ernie held in his teens occurred every third Saturday, when he drove Del Mar author Walt Coburn to get his hair cut in La Jolla. Coburn, whose best-known Western novel was "Barbed Wire", paid him $5.

"He owned two late-model Lincoln Zephyrs. One black. One white," Ernie said. "He'd been a genuine cowboy in Arizona and he'd roll out of the house in full Western gear with a silver belt buckle the size of a saucer."

Like many men in the 1930s Coburn rolled his own cigarettes, using Bull Durham tobacco." The cowboy slang for self-rolled was 'quorlies'," Ernie said. "Coburn lit his cigarettes by stretching out his leg to tighten his jeans and striking a match on his thigh."

Driving either one of the Zephyrs was a pleasure, Ernie said. Many times, as they glided along Highway 101, they wouldn't meet another car for ten minutes.

The only times being in a car wasn't fun for Ernie were the times his family were returning from seeing silent movies at The Granada, in La Jolla, where his Aunt Agnes played the organ.

"My father was my hero--but, bless his soul, he was the worst driver I've ever ridden with," he said. "To get home we had to go down the winding stretch of the old biological grade on Torrey Pines Road on the edge of the canyons. Dad would always stop at the top to change gears."

He can still hear, Ernie said, the screeching noise as his father wrestled the car into first. "Inside the car there'd be complete silence. We all knew what was coming. It took Dad at least ten minutes to inch the Maxwell down that grade."

<u>Footnote</u>: Ernie's father emigrated from Italy in 1905. His mom's grandfather was Don Juan Maria Osuna who, in the mid 1800s, owned 8,000 acres of land that became Rancho Santa Fe.

Nancy Ewing's book "Del Mar Looking Back" covers the intriguing history of both families.

CHAPTER SIXTEEN

" Captain Kenos "

Written April 2000

    In the 1950s Dave Young watched John Wayne break up a fight in the parking lot of Captain Keno's Encinitas restaurant. (It was called El Rancho then.)

"He sounded exactly like he did in the movies," Dave said of the 6-foot-4-inch actor. "He grabbed those two guys by their jacket collars, held them apart and drawled in that deep, slow voice, 'Okay, fellers, that's enough. We're going inside, and I'm gonna buy the house a drink'."

Captain Keno's--half bar, half restaurant--has topped the hill at 158 N. Highway 101 for nearly seventy years. It began as The Shamrock, was briefly Vienna Villa, and had a wild boom, followed by a thudding bust, as the El Rancho. It became Captain Keno's in 1970 when current owner Gerry Salvo celebrated getting the lease by gambling on Keno in Las Vegas.

"I was trying to make money," Gerry remembers. "But lost $100."

Gerry really needed money then. He opened his restaurant on a budget so tight—"I started with $550" he said--that he had to hitchhike from Vista every morning to open at 6 a.m. "I always carried a gas can because there was more chance of getting a ride."

In those days Gerry was twenty-nine, had black hair down to his waist and usually wore black silk Indian turbans. During his first eight months in business he did, literally, everything. "I'd tend bar when I had a customer there, and then dash over to the restaurant side and cook when I had customers there," he said.

At first there weren't many customers on either side. "So whenever I wasn't doing something I'd go outside, in my turban, and try to wave people in," he said.

As soon as he got a little money ahead Gerry bought seven old cars and parked them around his restaurant so people would think the place was packed. "Customers used to come in, glance around, and say,'Where is everybody?'" he remembers.

In the '30s and '40s, the Shamrock days, painted shamrocks covered the ceiling and north wall. "It was a roadhouse," said Bob Gooding, who played saxophone there with The Royal Four in the late '40s. "It was one of only a few between LA and Mexico, so the Hollywood crowd often stopped in on their way to and from Mexico."

Members of The Royal Four, who'd been classmates at San Dieguito High, had music stands with a crown and sepulcher on the front, and were all around nineteen. As well as Bob there was piano-player Tom Butts (whose parents owned Meadowlark Ranch) and two Del Mar boys--Tony Neiman on trombone and his cousin Jack on drums.

"We wore shirts and ties because there was no air conditioning in those days," Bob said.

The exact date when the Shamrock became El Rancho is debated locally, but Dave Young believes it was shortly before the '50s, when he and Bob Moffitt used to sing around the bar's piano.

"Which was played by a glamorous blonde named Shirley," he said. "We sang songs of the era, like 'Slow Boat to China'. Bob's voice was stronger, so he'd always lead and I'd harmonize."

Dave also remembers treating the dazzling Shirley to hamburgers in the coffee shop after the bar closed at 2 a.m. "Until one night her boy friend walked in and crushed my hopes."

On another night four union officials walked in. "They told the bartender, Shad, they'd smash the place up if the restaurant didn't join the union," Dave said. "Shad put one hand on the bar and leapt over. Half a dozen of us at the bar stood up and moved slowly towards those guys." The union men, he remembers, left hastily.

By the '50s El Rancho was in its heyday. "Open 24 hours a day," recalls John Kentera, who tended bar there in 1953 with another bartender known as Frenchie. "The restaurant was so busy people could hardly get in, and the coffee shop stayed open all night."

By this time the bar's pianist was Ron Coleman, moonlighting after his job at Encinitas Post Office. "Locals went there to have a good time," remembers Reba Brereton, whose husband, Booming Bill Brereton, sang love songs by the piano in a melodic tenor voice. (Bill was nicknamed "Booming" because he was a champion driver of midget race cars and the cars boomed as they came around the tracks.)

Then, in the mid '60s, the freeway siphoned away 101's traffic. "A lot of businesses didn't survive," John Kentera said.

El Rancho succumbed in 1966. For four years the restaurant on the hill stood empty--until Gerry Salvo came along.

These days Gerry, now a partner in five local businesses, lives in an apartment above Captain Keno's. He's still, in a way, waving people inside because every Thanksgiving and Christmas he throws a locally famous $3 holiday dinner. "It's for anybody who doesn't have anywhere to go," he said. "Doesn't matter if they're broke or they've got 10 million dollars. They're welcome."

CHAPTER SEVENTEEN

"George Bumann, Advice Remembered From a Pioneer Father."

Written July 1998

    Picture an isolated ranch in Olivenhain in the year 1917. Herman Bumann, a handsome man with a thick dark mustache, is hammering a loose board on the side of his barn. Close to him--as they often are--the youngest of his twelve children, George, aged four, and Bill, two and a half, are playing. The boys tumble around the dusty farmyard like overall-clad puppies. As George reaches his fingers into the feed chopper his small brother accidentally turns the machine on.
    "It's my earliest memory," George, now 85, said of the day he lost half of his left index finger. There was only one doctor in the North County then, Doctor

R.S. Reid, and he was in Oceanside. "On the buggy ride there, it was the first time I'd seen the ocean. I was far more interested in it than in my mutilated finger."

Today George is the only living person in our area whose parents were among the original Olivenhain pioneers.

His father, German tailor-turned-farmer Herman Bumann, arrived as a 22-year-old bachelor in November 1884. Deer roamed around his one-room shanty. The creek where he swam and watered his horse teemed with fish, water snakes, turtles. In 1893, by which time his one hundred and sixty acre homestead was a working farm, he married another German immigrant, Emma Marie Junker. Their marriage produced seven daughters, and five sons.

"Our home always had German traditions," George said. "At Christmas my mother hung cookies around the tree." (No candles, fire was something the pioneers, with their wooden homes and no piped-in water, really feared.). He remembers waking, every Christmas morning, to the sound of his father playing carols on the harmonica.

"Because Bill and I were his youngest he doted on us," George said. "In 1919 he bought an open touring car--the kind with a canvas hood you snap on if it rains--and he used to take us to San Diego with him, along nearly deserted roads. I still remember his advice to us. 'Never waste food. Never swear. And never, never feud with the neighbors'."

When Herman Bumann died, in 1926, he left four hundred and eighty acres of land, but not much money. "Our mother needed our help," George, who was nearly thirteen then , said. He and his older brother, Emil, ninteen, took over the care of Herman's apiary with its ninety five colonies of bees. They sold honey in five gallon cans. By the time he was sixteen George had $250 in savings in an Oceanside bank. (There wasn't a bank in the Encinitas area).

"One day, in the Fall of 1929, I went to the bank and it was locked up," George remembers. It was the first month of the Depression. A "Gone Out Of

Business" sign was taped to the bank's door. "My savings had gone with it. The same thing happened to many people then."

Some tough years followed. George spent six months sawing down dead trees for the Civilian Conservation Corps, who gave him $5 a month and sent $25 to his mother. But the rains of 1935 were a turning point.

The flowers bloomed. The bees flourished. "Emil and I earned so much from our honey I was able to buy my first house," he said. "On Barbara Street, in Solana Beach." He paid, he remembers, $930.

Things grew even brighter when, on a blind date in 1937, he met 17-year-old Rosemary Howard. (Rosemary was from Escondido, and George teased her about being a "Big City Girl".)

"We drove out to the Salton Sea in his brand new blue Ford," Rosemary remembers. "I thought he must be wealthy!"

Seven months later, when they returned from their Las Vegas honeymoon, George handed her a small book.

"What is it?" Rosemary asked.

She was astonished to learn it was a payment book for the Ford.

Life with George, Rosemary said, has been full of surprises, affection, and, occasionally, exasperation. He worked for the San Diego County Road Department for thirty-five years, bee-keeping on the side, but, like his father before him "landowning" runs in George Bumann's blood.

"In 1956 I was living happily in a beautiful house on Crest Drive in Cardiff," Rosemary said. "One day George drove me out to Olivenhain and showed me twenty acres of dusty bean fields. There wasn't a tree in sight. " The location was just up the road from where George had once been one of the twenty-eight pupils in Olivenhain's one-room schoolhouse.

"I want to buy this land," he told Rosemary. "And live here."

"I asked him if he'd gone mad," Rosemary remembers. "There was no water on the place. But he was so persuasive. He told our three children that if we moved out there we'd have horses. And cattle. And big dogs. I was outvoted four to one."

Today, forty-two years later, the Bumanns are still there, although they've sold off eighteen acres over the years. Eucalyptus, Pine and Pepper trees that George planted when they were about a foot high, loom above his lush fruit orchard. Dozens of different vegetables grow on ground that slopes towards the same creek where his pioneer father swam one hundred and fourteen years ago.

"Water was piped into Olivenhain in the early 1960s, and that made all the difference," explained George, who campaigned hard for it.

Most of the fruits and vegetables he grows he gives away to his neighbors. "That was good advice my father gave me for living a contented life," he said. "Never waste food. Never swear. And never, never feud with your neighbors."

CHAPTER EIGHTEEN

"Three Generations of McIntires Worked At Racetrack"

Written January 1999

    It was on a hot summer evening in 1936, as his father drove the family towards the beach at Del Mar, when 5-year-old Charlie McIntire noticed that the biggest building he'd ever seen was being built. Thick adobe walls (they were ten feet high) soared into the evening sky. A moat surrounded it.

"It was to become the Del Mar racetrack," Charlie said. "We passed it many times that summer, and I felt the same sense of awe Egyptian boys must have felt watching the pyramids rise."

Charlie's father, Charles W. McIntire, was, with a single partner, the only law enforcement officer in coastal North County during the mid-1930s and '40s.

"A deputy sheriff's pay was around $125 a month," Charlie said. "Not much for a man with a wife and three sons to support." In order to make ends meet his father wasn't averse, Charlie suspects, to taking the occasional bribe. Or the not-so-occasional one. "Once a fisherman dumped a whole truck load of frozen albacore on our front lawn at three in the morning," he said. "My parents worked all that day, and well into the next night, cooking and canning all that fish."

In the 1940s Sheriff Mac, as the locals called him, began doubling-up, working at the race track every season. He'd patrol his own "beat" during the day, the racetrack at night, one of four deputies under Captain Earl Riley. Long hours never seemed to bother his father, Charlie said. "In summer he was always smiling."

Charlie's own work experience at the track began in 1947. Just sixteen, six feet tall and a skinny one hundred and forty pounds, his boss at Anderson-Dunham, the track's catering contractor, nicknamed him "Slippery".

In those days, racegoers reached the upper levels of the grandstand by a ramp with a ninety-degree turn. A few days into the season "Slippery" was trying to impress his boss by wheeling a cart overloaded with crates of empty beer bottles down the ramp, when the cart careened out of control. "I hung on, horrified," he said. "Fans were climbing the ramp, their noses buried in racing forms." Fortunately several cases crashed from the cart, alerted fans flattened themselves against the walls, and the cart struck only one person, a heavyset woman.

"I'm amazed I wasn't fired," Charlie said. "Instead they switched me to washing dishes in the main hall until midnight." (Years later he learned the woman struck by the cart had been awarded $40,000 damages.)

The next summer was easier. Charlie became one of the track's parking valets, employed by the Del Mar Turf Club.

"These were coveted jobs. It was before tips had to be declared for taxes," he said. "Some of the guys who worked valet parking for years became wealthy men. The most lucrative spot was the trainers and owners lot. "I've seen valets stashing their tips in the club safe because their pockets were bulging." His own station, though, near the Don Diego Tower, wasn't a place for big tippers.

"Every day I'd see about 200 men, mostly elderly, hanging around," he remembers. " I couldn't understand why, as soon as the gates opened at 11, they'd rush in, racing each other! But someone explained that any seat a big winner had sat in previously was considered 'lucky'."

One serious problem at the track, Charlie said, was that locals weren't wanted. "The guys who traveled the circuit--Santa Anita, Hollywood Park, etc.--conspired to give us the worst jobs, hoping we'd quit and the job would go to one of their northern buddies."

One night the guard who manned the remote gate in the stable area was killed while crossing Highway 101. Charlie was offered the job. "I decide not to fight the move," he said. "Of the eleven locals I'd started with I was the only one left. Being a stable gateman was one of the least desirable jobs on the track, so I figured they'd leave me alone."

Charlie kept on working at the track through his college years at San Diego State University. He missed a few seasons while in the Navy, but returned in

1957, the same year he began his thirty-four year career teaching social studies for San Dieguito High School in Encinitas.

"For a while teaching and the track worked out beautifully together," he remembers. "But then school began starting earlier and earlier. Sometimes a week would overlap. I'd be changing from suit to uniform in the nearest bathroom, zooming between school and track, on my motorcycle."

Charlie retired from teaching in 1991, but not from the track. Now Stable Superintendent, he starts preparing in June; assigning stable slots to trainers. He works from a vast map where places the public rarely sees, such as the horse hospital, and the shoeing room, are marked. Each season he's responsible for finding accommodations for around 2,500 horses and 1,500 people.

"Del Mar's unique, the only track in America that's also a fairground," he said. "It's a tremendous amount of work getting all the carny stuff out, ripping up floor boards and putting earth put down for the stables."

Fifteen years ago Lollie McIntire, Charlie's daughter, became the track's first, and only, female stable gate guard. "It wasn't easy for her. She joined the union and hung on," Charlie says of Lollie, whose all-year-round job is managing banquets at La Costa Resort and Spa.

Which makes her the third generation McIntire to work at the adobe-walled track her father gazed at in awe that hot summer of 1936.

CHAPTER NINETEEN

"Dr. Harry Hill, First Encinitas Vet to Open Small Animal Practice"

Written September 2000

"Anyone who has read James Herriot's books knows that working with large animals can be hazardous," said Dr. Harry Hill, who has a crooked finger on his right hand as a souvenir of a lively dentistry session on a horse.

When he first began practicing veterinary medicine in Encinitas, in the early 1950s, Harry's large animal work included such highlights as nights with Charlie Miller's cows.

"Charlie and I would be out there in a field, usually around 3 a.m., trying to deliver a calf with both of us lying on our bellies in manure," he remembers. "In those days Charlie, who owned the feed store in downtown Encinitas, had cows in several fields along north El Camino Real."

But it was an experience with one of Tex Wimer's horses that persuaded Harry to limit his practice to small animals.

Tex Wimer had stables on the Rancho Santa Fe side of La Bajada Creek. "He kept four or five horses that he'd rent to riders," Harry said. "One night I was examining a horse and, while my arm was inside the horse's lower bowel, he backed me into a corner. I felt a strong contraction, and knew what was coming."

"Tex! Take her forward!" Harry yelled.

He'd time, he remembers, for one more "Tex!" before the horse showered him with excrement.

"From somewhere in the stable I heard Tex's voice drawl, very slowly, 'Y'okay back there, Doc?'"

Harry's small animal practice, the first one in the Encinitas area, opened in the mid '50s in Leucadia, at 222 N.Highway 101. (The red and white barn-shaped building is still there, next to Marci's Flowers.)

"There were no sophisticated diagnostic tools, like ultra sound and cat scans, then," he said. "To discover what was wrong with an animal you had four things. Your hands, your thermometer, your stethoscope and your mind."

He came out of veterinary school feeling he knew everything, Harry said. But when his first patient, a black cocker spaniel, walked in with his master, Harry's mind went blank.

"I thought, My God, I've got a client who wants me to find out what's wrong with his animal! Someone who is going to pay me! Finally I remembered to take the dog's temperature. That broke the spell."

Harry was originally a Navy Brat, born on Coronado Island in 1923. By the war years he was in the Navy himself and part of a group of young people who partied at the Encinitas "Casino". It was at the Casino that he courted his first wife, Bonnie Jean Truax, who, while at San Dieguito High, shared the nickname, with her twin sister Betty Jo, of "The Dynamite Duo".

"The Casino was our name for Lyle Hammond's apartment," Harry said. "It was right next-door to the La Paloma Theatre and there was a party going on there just about every night. It sounds wild, but it wasn't. This was before pot and the strongest thing we drank was beer." Usually, he said, they'd sit around listening to the radio." Then Lyle--we all called him Pop--would start strumming his ukulele. Mac Brink would play the piano and we'd sing songs like "My Blue Heaven".

No matter what songs they sang, Harry said, they always ended up singing one that Lyle wrote, which began "It happened on the beach in Encinitas."

In 1948 UC Davis opened a veterinary school, and Harry went through on the GI Bill, graduating in 1952 with the charter class. By the time he opened the small animal practice in Leucadia he was happy to specialize in cats and dogs, he said, with the occasional exotic creature.

"Once George Weber brought in a dead iguana and said he'd been having trouble getting it to eat," he recalled. "We opened the box and it was lying there-- but iguanas always freeze. I picked him up to look at his mouth and the whole iguana came up stiff as a board. 'George," I said."I think your iguana is no longer with us.' "

In the '50s the restaurant/bar closest to Harry's surgery was the El Rancho (now Captain Keno's) where Jerry Hammond, Lyle Hammond's son, had painted the walls on two sides with Western scenes of cattle herding.

"The late '40s, early '50s were the days when both the El Rancho and Cardiff's Beacon Inn had live music," Harry said. "The musicians moved back and forth between the two."

"In the '50s, when TV came to Encinitas, we used to watch the Friday night boxing matches on a very small screen--which looked big to us--over the El Rancho's bar. Sometimes the fights in the bar were more entertaining than the ones on TV."

Although he's had many pets of his own--including a cat called El Fugitivo that his then wife smuggled over the Mexican border in a paper bag--Harry's favorite animal, he said, will always be the Jack Russell Terrier. He's spent several "vacations" planting tracking devices in kangaroos in the Australian outback and has been chased by an elephant in Kenya. After nearly fifty years as a vet he still works with animals four days a week at Solana Beach's Academy Animal Hospital.

His close friend Penelope Grant has a story about Harry that illustrates what it's like to work as a vet in one community for nearly fifty years.

"About a dozen years ago Harry and I were shopping in the old Thrifty Drug store on Santa Fe Drive," Penelope said. "A woman kept staring at him. Finally she came over to him and said, 'Didn't you used to be Dr. Harry Hill?' "

CHAPTER TWENTY

"Floods, Coyotes, and Amorous Turkeys"

Written January 1999

    Perhaps you've noticed the old Teten house? It sits by itself, crumbling gently below its peaked red roof, on land at the corner of Encinitas Boulevard and Vulcan Avenue in Encinitas. Next time you pass the place it may enliven your trip to picture it as a thriving turkey farm.
    John and Laura Anna Teten raised thousands of turkeys while living in that house. Numerous times John dashed out into the night (he slept in the kind of long underwear that has a flap in the back) clutching his shotgun because a coyote was raiding the turkey pens.

John Teten married Laura Anna Bumann, (daughter of Olivenhain pioneer Herman Bumann), in 1917. They had four children: Viola Annie, Evelyn, Gladys, and Roger, but Viola Annie drowned when she was only nineteen months old. It was Gladys born in 1926 and now Mrs. Schull, who gave me a vivid picture of what it was like to grow up surrounded by turkeys.

"Grandpa Fred, Dad's father, who was a blacksmith, originally built the house in Olivenhain around 1892," she said. "It was on Rancho Santa Fe Road then. Mother gave birth to all of us in the back bedroom there."

The turkeys, she remembers, were hard work. The Tom turkeys mated at every available chance they got, and to protect the females from getting ripped by sharp claws, Laura Anna kept them dressed in "turkey saddles"; a kind of canvas vest through which the bird's wings poked. The childrens' chores included herding the turkeys into their pens at night (they'd fly up in trees and be difficult to get down) feeding the mules, horses, pigs and chickens, milking the cows, collecting the eggs, hoeing the weeds between the rows of lima beans their father raised and stacking the beans.

"Whenever it rained all the bean stacks had to be turned over to prevent mildew," Gladys remembers. "One year it rained and rained. Our neighbor on the hill above us, Bruno Denk, had built a dam to hold water and the dam broke. We were all floundering about in the flood water trying to scoop up turkeys as they washed towards the creek."

The creek, she explained, was always a source of fun.

"There was no one around to see us, so we usually swam naked. Another thing we did for fun was to make our own cigarettes from corn silk rolled in newspaper and smoke them behind the barn. Dad smoked Bull Durham, which came in cloth bags, and we'd always shake out these bags in case any tobacco was left." Roger, she remembers, started making cigarettes when he was only six. "I don't know how the barn survived!"

The Teten children also enjoyed their one-room Olivenhain school. "It was like having private tutoring," Gladys said. In the 1930s the teacher, Martha Wiro, had an enrollment of nine, which soon dropped to five. "She could fit the whole school into her car for field trips and we went everywhere--the San Diego Fair, the tuna factory, the missions."

Their most ambitious field trip, Gladys said, was the Amtrack's first run in May 1938. "It was called the Streamline Train then. We got all dressed up in hats and gloves and rode from Oceanside to San Diego to see the just-built Civic building."

At home on the farm Gladys remembers a steady stream of housewives--"Some even arrived in chauffeur-driven cars from as far away as La Jolla,"--who came for her mother's cream, butter and eggs. But Thanksgiving, and particularly Christmas, were, she said, "difficult times at our house."

John Teten always killed the turkeys with a swift knife blow to the brain. He and the hired men took care of the feather-plucking, but it was Laura Anna who gutted and dressed them for customers. "The day before Christmas our kitchen would be full of galvanized tubs of guts, turkeys hanging everywhere, turkeys on every chair because there was no place left to put them," Gladys said. "But on Christmas day the house would be clean and Mother would produce a wonderful dinner. I don't know how she did it."

In November 1940 Laura Anna was rushed to the hospital. A tumor had burst and she'd developed peritonitis. Evelyn was away in college by then and Roger was needed for the outside work. That Christmas the whole business of de-gutting, of life among the galvanized tubs, fell to 14-year-old Gladys. "Somehow I got through," she said.

Evelyn Teten Richard died in her fifties. These days Gladys lives in Oceanside, and so does Roger and his wife, Jeanette. The old farmhouse built by "Grandpa Fred" will become, along with its original furniture, a part of a soon-to-be-built historical park in Encinitas. If you're a Teten, though, it means occasionally being asked if you still keep turkeys.

"No way!" Roger Teten said firmly. "The only time I like to have contact with a turkey now is out of the oven, with rich stuffing."

CHAPTER TWENTY ONE

"King Brothers' Business began in Back Yard Shed"

Written January 2001

When you read this you may wonder if Jim King was pulling my leg about the size of the pipes into which his agile father wriggled. Jim swears they were 20-inch and 18-inch ones, and he's such a respectable citizen I'd never dispute him!

The scene is a warm Sunday afternoon, in the early 1940s. The stretch of Encinitas Boulevard that soars up from El Camino Real hasn't been named yet; but is known locally as "Red Hill". Dusty sage brush flanks its narrow sides.

Three 15-year-old boys, Jim King, Paul Ecke Jr., and Chuck Larrick, are rattling down Red Hill in an aging Model A.

"It was my first car, bought for $10," Jim King recalls. "I never went anywhere in it without taking a coat hanger along for mechanical repairs."

They were half way down the hill that day, Jim said, "When the engine blew up. A rod hurtled straight through the side and into the sage brush." The three boys stood in the road, peering into a hole through which the engine's works showed clearly. Obviously this was a job that went far beyond the coat hanger's capabilities.

"Well...the engine's still running," Chuck said. "We could try driving home?"

"Once we started we didn't dare stop," Jim remembers. "Oil was flying out. When we reached the Ecke's ranch, on Saxony Road, Paul leapt from the car. Chuck and I made it home to Solana Beach just before the oil ran dry."

Jim has loved cars--particularly Model As--as long as he can remember. Many longtime locals, though, associate him with the Culligan soft water plant that he, his older brother, Bob, and their father, built on Solana Beach's Cedros Avenue in 1951.

Jim was two in 1928 when his parents, Ernest and Lillian King, moved to Rancho Santa Fe. Ernest had been loaned by Vista Irrigation District to Santa Fe Irrigation to repair some of their pipes. He was supposed to be with them two weeks, and stayed thirty one years.

"Dad was a small, very strong man. He could crawl inside twenty inch, even eighteen inch pipes," Jim said. "In 1929, when the Great Depression hit, there were five men on Dad's crew, each making $100 a month." The manager told them that one of them had to go, or all five could stay and take a cut to $80. "Without hesitation they agreed to the cut," Jim said. "To have a job in those days was really something."

In 1930 the five Kings--Bob was three years older than Jim, his sister Pat, the baby of the family, a year younger--moved to Solana Beach to a house on Rios. (The Solana Beach Fish House restaurant sits on that spot now.) Their landlord, Duke Wilkens, charged $17.50 a month rent and, except for Duke's garden supply store on the corner, they had the use of the whole acreage where the shopping center is now.

"There was plenty of room for an orchard, cow, chickens, ducks and rabbits. As well as a large vegetable garden, and a ball field," Jim said.

During the Depression children took whatever work was available, and Jim remembers his brother, at ten, going to work in the ironworks on Cedros. (The building now houses Elements furniture store.)

"It was also a blacksmith's shop. The anvil and forge were still there in the 30s," Jim said. "Bob spent his first day drilling hundreds of tiny holes in sprinkler heads."

"I've never had such a boring job!" Bob announced at the dinner table.

"That's the only job you've ever had," Ernest pointed out.

The King family had been living in the house on Rios for ten years when Duke Wilkens decided it would be reasonable to raise the rent a dollar a month, to $18.50. His father, Jim said, didn't feel this was at all reasonable. "He and Mother went up the hill and bought a house on the corner of Lirio and Via de Vista. Their mortgage was $25 a month, nothing down."

The Lirio house had two bedrooms. "My parents had one, Pat the other, and Bob and I slept in a wooden shed Dad built in the back yard. After a few months we got high falutin' and lined the walls with cardboard," Jim said. By this time his mother was working at the telephone company in Del Mar--where operators often listened to calls--motivating a teenage Jim to use the phone at the drugstore.

Ernest King had always taken jobs on the side. He'd fix washing machines, install sprinkler systems, and repair pipes. In 1946, Bob and Jim, aged twenty-three and twenty and recently back from World War II, were helping their Dad with a job in Rancho Santa Fe.

"The customer had saved us a tiny advertisement from Life magazine," Jim said. "All it said was,'Culligan soft water franchises available', with a number to call."

They had a vague idea of what soft water was, he said, and they certainly knew what dirty water was. (San Dieguito didn't have a filtration plant until 1970. Longtimers tell stories of weeds coming out of their taps.)

The King family's Culligan franchise was launched in 1946, with Bob and Jim working out of a small shed in their back yard--a metal one this time. Their Dad helped in his spare time, and their mother was their office manager for thirteen years.

"As business grew we built the plant on Cedros ourselves, block by block. It took us about a year and a half," Jim remembers. It was finished in '51, the same year he married Encinitas-born Janie Phillips.

"In our garage there's a Model A that Jim gave me for my birthday, thirty-five years ago," Janie said. In those days all three of their children, Jim Jr., Teri and Nancy, could fit into the Model A's rumble seat, she said. "We used to drive it out to Escondido for ice cream at Baskin Robbins, and, always, we took along a coat hanger."

CHAPTER TWENTY TWO

"Olivenhain's Pioneer Cemetery"

Written July 1998

    Back in 1917, when young Olivenhain farmer Bruno Denk was courting a beautiful, fair-haired girl named Alwine, he used to zoom up to her house on his motorcycle bringing her bunches of shooting star flowers.
    "Shooting Stars grew wild then. They were all over this cemetery. Tidytip daisies, too. But they've disappeared now," Harley Denk, who is Bruno and Alwine's son, says as I follow him up the hill where Olivehain's cemetery sprawls across two and a half acres. It's a peaceful place. On this summer

morning the only sounds, other than our voices, are birds and the crunch-crackle of pine needles under our shoes.

On the small gravestones--no ostentatious marble angels soaring on this hill--I notice the same names again and again. Wiro. Teten. Scott. Lux. Cole. Ewing. I count sixteen Bumanns. (Sometimes with one 'M', sometimes two). Olivenhain families have buried their dead here since the days of the first settlers. To be buried here now, though, you have to have lived in Olivenhain since at least 1975 or, as in the case of Martha Wiro whose ashes were flown back from Australia, have reserved your spot.

As I crunch along behind Harley--who inherited part of the land the cemetery is on from his father, and who keeps handwritten burial records in a 114-year-old ledger--I keep recognizing names of people I've written about for this column.

"There's Christiana Wiegand!" I exclaim. "I'll always remember that she fed cactus to her cattle."

During draught years, Harley tells me, the early settlers also fed seaweed to their cattle. "They got by any way they could. They'd ride their horses over to the beaches and dig up clams to stretch the hog feed," he says as we pause by a weathered redwood-fenced square. Herman Hauk, Harley's maternal grandfather, is buried in the square, along with his two wives.

Amelia Hauck, the first wife, was also the first person to be buried in the cemetery, at the age of twenty-nine, in 1891. Her's is the only grave that faces north. The second wife, Alwine, died only four years later, while giving birth to a daughter. (The baby, named after her mother, grew up to be the girl Bruno Denk courted with shooting star flowers.)

"In those early years winter burials were hard because there wasn't a paved road up here," Harley says. "The horses pulling the wagon with the coffin often had to struggle through thick mud. My grandfather died in winter and I remember my dad telling me they had to dig a trench from the grave to drain out the water."

Summer burials, he adds, weren't much easier." The soil is adobe, very hard. And graves had to be dug at least six feet down to avoid bad smells because--let's be realistic--there was no embalming then."

As late as 1950, he says, the graves were all dug by hand. "Sweaty, skin-blistering work. It took a dozen men, using picks and shovels and taking turns, an entire day. Now we bring in a back hoe and it takes half an hour."

Harley and I move on, passing more names. Eckhardt. Laugher. Ingersol. Reseck. Muse. Fist-sized gopher holes pock the uneven ground, and the scent of pine hangs heavily in the warm air. There's no caretaker here. Once a year, on the Saturday before Memorial Day, volunteers descend on the cemetery with hoes and rakes and weed-whackers. The place is run as a non-profit corporation. "With a board of seven directors, two changed each year," Harley explains. He points out what will be his own final resting place, beside his first wife Rose (a Ewing) although he's now remarried to a cheerful lady named Mary to whom all this Olivenhain history is new.

The cemetery's "mystery grave" belongs to a distant relative of Harley's, and sits on the South slope. Paul Lehman, once Governor of New York, assumed his brother's identity when the brother was killed by a billiard stick. "So the story goes, anyway," Harley says. "If true, that's the brother lying down there."

Only a few of the gravestones have inlaid carving. A small bird, a robin, graces the one that says only "Baby Scott". Below the name "Pop" Herman Wiegand's stone shows the outline of a man in a cowboy hat riding a horse.

And on the grave of William "Bill" Wiro, who was born shortly after his parents emigrated here from Germany and who, in 1916, livened up local conversation considerably by eloping with Marie Bumann, is the simple message "Widersenn".

"People were very neighborly then," Harley says. "They joined together to harvest crops, to build barns. We don't have that any more." He glances down the hill, towards where, invisible beyond the trees, Encinitas throbs with traffic and construction-in-progress. He was born in 1921, he says, and remembers when there were sweeping golden fields of barley there. "As far as you could see. When they harvested it, the wild pink flowers were left close to the ground. Overnight the fields turned from golden to pink."

As Harley and I leave the cemetery I glance back at the tranquil hillside and think how hard all these people must have worked. Having been such good neighbors, they are, in a way, now neighbors for ever.

Chiseled into the stone where Alwin Wiegand lies beside his wife Frieda are words that seem particularly apt for Olivenhain's early settlers.

"Each duty done they rest in peace."

CHAPTER TWENTY THREE

"The Danforth Building"

Written October 1998

My son Craig and his wife, Jen, live in the Danforth building, and the illustrations for this book were created there. The Danforth was built in 1916, making it, today, the oldest apartment building in Encinitas. Although it's a fun place to live--like stepping back in time--and rare tilework decorates the stairs, Craig and

Jen's apartment does have its drawbacks. "Including the original plumbing," Jen says. "Whenever we take a shower we listen for the foghorn groaning noise that warns us we've two seconds to leap out before the water turns boiling."

If you've driven along the 500 block of South Coast Highway 101, you've probably stopped right next to the Danforth Building--9 apartments upstairs, 6 shops underneath--at the E Street Stoplight.

In 1940, when Eckka Rowe bought the building, those were the only stoplights in town.

Strong-willed Eckka, the nation's first female engineer, and her quiet husband George, an expert on agriculture, had lost their San Diego property during the Depression. The down payment for the Encinitas building was all that remained from a relative fortune of $300,000 that Eckka's father, an inventor, had left her in 1916.

"They moved into the upstairs apartment on the South corner," John Danforth said of his grandparents. "And collected rents from the rest of the building to pay the mortgage." The building's stores, he said, were pretty typical of a small American town. "They included the post office, a soda fountain that sold bus tickets, a barber shop, dress shop, Halstead's 5 & 10 and a market."

In 1942, John, aged nine, and his younger brother Pete, seven, were sent to live with their grandparents. (Their mother, Jane, was Eckka and George's daughter).

"We'd been living in Kensington, San Diego. At his Army medical Dad was suspected of having tuberculosis. He didn't, but until they knew for sure our parents were worried we'd be infected too," John remembers. "And mom was working long hours at a wartime job as a draftsman--draftsperson you'd say now--at Convair."

101, as the Coast Highway was called, was the only road between Los Angeles and San Diego. It rumbled with traffic, even back then. The boys spent hours peering down from their grandparent's kitchen window, counting the cars that stopped at the traffic light.

"There was a gun embankment on the end of E Street, and after school a bunch of us would walk along the cliffs to visit marines sitting in dugouts." Pete Danforth remembers. The marines, he said, were watching for enemy activity. "But the enemy never got around to Encinitas."

Other after-school diversions included rolling about in hay behind Miller's Feed Store.--"Charlie Miller had so much hay back there he never noticed us," John said -- and body-surfing at Moonlight Beach.

"There was a great guy named Bill Hipsley down at Moonlight. He rented out balloon-like rafts, soft as pillows," Pete said. "They cost twenty five cents an hour, but if you didn't have the money he'd let you take one anyway, and say, 'Don't tell anyone.' "

Only four years later their beach-time dwindled dramatically when their parents, Ben and Jane Danforth, took over the Encinitas Market. The grocery business was one of the Danforth Building's six stores.

"Our parents needed all the after-school help we could manage," Pete said. (It worked out well later, though, as both John and Pete used skills they'd learned in Encinitas Market to help pay their way through college.)

Although the war was over in 1946, food rationing still lingered." The people who ran the market before us had gone off without leaving any ration coupons," said John, who turned thirteen that year. "You couldn't buy meat, sugar, soap powder, lots of things, without them."

"Whenever a customer would come in asking for sugar, Mom would slip me one of our own coupons. I'd run across the street to the Safeway, bring back sugar, and Mom would sell it to the customer in exchange for one of their coupons."

Customers, John said, knew what was going on. "But this was such a friendly town, people just went along with it for the month or so it took us to build up coupons."

He earned ten cents an hour for working with his mother on the grocery side, he said. "Pete worked on the butcher's counter with Dad, for five cents!"

"Dad knew nothing about being a butcher," Pete said. "But there was a preacher, with a church over on Vulcan, who'd been one. He taught Dad, who more or less learned on the job."

In those days, Pete explained, meat wasn't set out in plastic-wrapped packages. "We cut to order. One day I was at the counter by myself when the actor Pat O'Brian walked in and asked for lamb chops. I didn't have any to give him. I was so disappointed I've never forgotten it!"

Jane Danforth inherited the building when her mother died after owning it for twenty years. The inheritance passed on to her sons--with other property going to her daughters Caroline and Christine--when Jane herself died seven years ago.

"It was built in 1916, and not much more than patching had ever been done to it," John said of the building he and his brother are currently restoring. "We're very aware that downtown Encinitas has a character all its own. We're trying to keep the best features, like the hardwood floors, the high ceilings, and improve the worst, like the antique plumbing."

If you're driving past you may notice signs saying two new businesses are about to be launched in the old-new Danforth. There's Crystal Wells' "Detour" hair salon, and Sarah Rosenfield's boutique "Sangria". In a way you could say they're updated versions--well, okay, very updated versions--of the barber shop and dress shop Eckka Rowe collected the rent from in 1940.

CHAPTER TWENTY FOUR

"Herman Wiegand and The Talking Machine "

Written September 1999

    In May 1896 a stranger driving a horse and buggy drew up outside Olivenhain's one-room schoolhouse. He strode inside carrying a large wooden box with a handle on one end, a horn on the other.

"He told us it was Edison's invention, a talking machine" Herman Wiegand recalled in a letter written when he was ninety eight. That day in the schoolhouse Herman was a round-faced, blond 6-year-old who watched and listened, enthralled, as the stranger cranked the machine's handle. Powered by clockwork, a needle dropped onto a cylinder and the story of Sherman's march through Georgia rattled scratchily from the horn.

"Tomorrow you'll hear songs," the man promised. "Bring five cents for each recording."

Herman, his sister Elizabeth and big brother, Alwin, raced home to their German Immigrant parents' farm in Aliso Canyon, now part of Rancho Santa Fe.

"Songs? Ach--this you do not need," their father, Adam Wiegand, told them. (Adam loved his five children, but was so frugal that once, when a dangerous bull knocked him down, he yelled to Herman, "Don't shoot it, it cost too much money!")

"Next day in school all the kids but the three Wiegands brought nickels and quarters," recalled Herman, who, ninety-two years later, still vividly remembered his disappointment.

The story of Herman's life, growing up in the first decade of this century, often sounds like a Western movie. In 1913, when an epidemic of Blackleg--a disease fatal to young cattle--was rampaging through California he rode for twenty-four hours, from dawn to dawn, to bring a vaccine from Ramona.

By this time the Wiegand's home farm was on five hundred acres of land in Olivenhain, close to where Manchester Avenue runs today. Christiana Wiegand, Herman's mother, cooked wonderful meals there, and prayed her children wouldn't fall into ungodly ways. Dancing, Christiana felt, definitely fell into this category. Herman was around nineteen when she hid his side-buttoned boots, and those of his younger brother Fritz, to prevent her boys going to a dance.

Olivenhain didn't have a church, but a young Lutheran minister named Louis Meyer made the four-hour trip from Escondido every other Sunday afternoon. He preached in the schoolhouse, so Herman was sitting in almost the same spot where he'd listened to Edison's talking machine when he first saw the minister's 22-year-old sister. Her name was Mary Johanna.

Herman courted her with bunches of white Shooting Star flowers, wearing a $12.95 suit. He loved her for the rest of his life.

They were married in 1914, when they were both twenty-four. In the tradition of the pioneer families, Herman's father, the frugal Adam, not only gave them several hundred acres of land, but built them a house, too.

Herman was already a veteran cattleman by then (He'd bought his first cow when he was only ten, but unfortunately it died the next day). He began building a herd of white-faced cattle that, over the years, would grow to around five hundred. As he believed that a man's word is his bond, he rarely signed contracts. Often, he bought or sold his cattle on the strength of only a handshake.

In 1916 Herman and Mary's first child, a son, was stillborn.

Their second baby, Mildred, was always delicate. So when Mary Ann arrived, in 1920, six years before the last child, Bill, she quickly became Herman's "little cowgirl helper."

"Pops would often ride his mustang all day taking care of the cattle, and I'd jiggle along behind on my pony, Dandy," Mary Ann remembers. "My legs got so numb Mother used to rub them before we sat down to supper."

She was seven the day she came home from school to find the doctor's car in the yard. "Shhh, be very quiet," her mother warned. "Pops has had an accident."

"He'd been 'dallying'--which means the rope holding a cow is wound around the pommel of the saddle," Mary Ann said. "A large cow had bolted, wrenching the rope so tightly it pulled off his right thumb. He told me that in those days lacking a thumb was considered the sign of a true cowboy!"

Mary Johanna died in 1969. Twenty years later Herman wrote in his diary that there had never been a day when he hadn't missed her. He kept working his cattle ranch until his eighties, and riding until his late nineties. When he died he'd spent one hundred and three years living in this area; ninety-two of them riding horses.

Mary Ann took a photograph of her father riding his favorite horse, Tekla, to the man who carved his gravestone. "And you can see it's him," she says of the carving. The stone sits on a quiet hill in Olivenhain's Pioneer Cemetery, and says simply,

"Pop. Herman August Wiegand 1890 - 1993. He's gone home".

Footnote: The talking machine that Herman listened to as a child was the earliest record player, the phonograph, invented by Thomas Alva Edison in 1877. Edison was deaf at the time, but registered the sound vibrations on tinfoil.

CHAPTER TWENTY FIVE

" When The North County Waited For An Enemy Invasion"

Written September 1999

When Bob Gooding told me about the World War II plan to drop exploding bats on Japan I thought, as I had when Jim King told me about his father crawling through those narrow pipes, that perhaps I was being kidded. (Followed by the thought, gosh, those poor little bats!) But after this column came out I had calls from several people who were involved in this top-secret plan, including one man who had helped to manufacture the cages in Solana Beach.

My earliest memory, at three, is of a night in England during World War II when the banshee wail of an air raid warning ripped the air, and several prostitutes turned up at my grandparents' home. (My grandfather always called them "Fallen Flowers.") They came because the cellar there was handy as a neighborhood bomb shelter.

My grandmother, born in the prudish reign of Queen Victoria, stood on the stairs, one hand clutching her lace collar. "Delia!" she said to my mother, "Those women? Are they....are they what I think they are......?"

Mum, towing me towards a bed in the cellar, glanced back and exclaimed, "For heavens sakes, Mother, there's a war on!"

Here in the North County the only World War II bomb shelters I've heard about are the bunkers that are rumored to be underneath Del Mar's fairgrounds. But, from President Roosevelt's radio announcement about Pearl Harbor on December 8th, 1941 to the day Japan surrendered, on August 14th, 1945, most people expected an enemy invasion.

If you lived here then, you learned to cover your windows at night with black cloth so that not a chink of light could be glimpsed by enemy ships or planes. Coast guards patrolled the beaches with dogs, and soldiers watched the ocean from a cement fortress on the bluffs near Moonlight Beach. Another fortress--they were called "pillboxes"--stood on the bluffs above Solana Beach's Fletcher Cove. A huge blimp, which was kept tethered between use at a base at Del Mar's fairgrounds, could be seen hovering above the sea, searching for enemy submarines.

"My father was past the draft age," Bob Grice remembers. "So he joined the Civil Defense and guarded the railroad bridge at Del Mar, carrying a wooden gun."

As far as anyone knows the closest the Japanese ever got to the North County was to lob a few shells from a submarine at some oil tankers a few miles west of Santa Barbara.

"But we reported every plane we saw or heard flying over, just to be sure," said George Wilkens, who was one of the North County's volunteer "spotters." George, who was twenty when Pearl Harbor was attacked, got married shortly before he was drafted into the Army. In the early months of 1942 he and his bride, Jean, spent many nights plane-spotting, huddled with a thermos of coffee and a field telephone on top of Del Mar's water tower.

These were the years of v-mail from overseas, which arrived, censored, in flimsy beige envelopes: of posters urging women to "Get a War Job! Longing won't bring him back sooner." Everything from shoes, to coffee, to rubber tires was rationed, and a Government warning of "Ten years in prison for violations" was printed on the ration coupon books.

Sugar was particularly hard to get. So Olivenhain-born brothers Emil and George Bumann managed, as well as working full-time for the County Road Department, to extract up to a thousand five-gallon cans of honey a year from their bee hives.

"I still bake with honey instead of sugar," Rosemary Bumann, George's wife, said.

"We were never short of food because of all the farms this area had then," said Herb Lux, who grew up on a farm on Cardiff's Manchester Avenue. Farmers, most of whom had gas pumps on their land, received extra gasoline rations. "They had underground tanks holding several hundred gallons," Herb said. "It was supposed to be only for tractors, but there were a lot of cars that filled up at those tractor pumps."

"For the small children 'Daddy' was often only a face in a photograph," said Maggie Wolfe, whose son, Dennis, was born on the same day her husband,

Curly, was drafted." I used to visit the men stationed at the blimp base, to invite them to Del Mar's USO. Most of them were really missing their children, so I started taking Dennis with me. They were wonderful to him."

The most bizarre story I heard about North County's war years involved exploding bats. In the mid '40s a man named Cubic, who lived on Cardiff's Mackinnon Avenue, designed a special cage for the Department of Defense.

"He worked, in top secret, inside one of the buildings the WPA built at the Del Mar fairgrounds," said Bob Gooding, whose father was a friend of Cubic's. Bob saw the actual plans for this cage when he was seventeen. "It was huge," he said. "Image a giant bird house, about the size of a dinner table, with numerous doors designed to open on impact."

In those days there was an airport beside the fairgrounds. The plan, Bob said, was that bats would be flown in from Carlsbad Caverns in New Mexico. When weather conditions were exactly right, each bat would have an incendiary device fastened around its neck. The cage of bats would then be flown over Japan and dropped. The next stage, if all went according to plan, was that the bats would fly under the eves of Japanese houses, explode on impact, and touch off a fire storm.

"Cubic never did get to launch his bomber bats," Bob said. "Right about the time he was ready to go, the atomic bomb was dropped on Hiroshima."

CHAPTER TWENTY SIX

"Bill Arballo"

Written April 2000

Newspaperman Bill Arballo was Del Mar's 5th mayor. This column about his boyhood seemed to follow naturally after the chapter about waiting for an enemy invasion.

If there was a prize for the most intriguing bit of local history-mystery, I'd definitely award it to Bill Arballo.

It happened early in 1941, when Bill, sixteen, was fishing on the beach at Del Mar with his older sister, Mary, and younger brother, Bobby. "We noticed a short, thin man, who looked Japanese, standing on the edge of the water," Bill said. "He seemed lost. Except for a loincloth, he was naked, and apparently didn't speak a word of English."

The three Arballo children felt they couldn't just leave him there, shivering. "So we took him home, found him something to wear, and he lived in our garage for two weeks, " Bill said. "We fed him tortillas and beans."

Had he come off a submarine? Was he a spy?

"We never found out," Bill said. " Mary did manage to discover that he was a map-maker, but soon after that he slipped away."

Del Mar was a quiet, beautiful backwater then. The town only had three hundred and fifty people when, in 1933, widower Loreto Arballo arrived with his children, aged ten, eight and six, in a 1924 Model-T that, Bill remembers, "Would only go backwards up steep hills."

"My father, born in Mexico, was a farmer who planted by the moon," "Bill said. "He worked for Solana Beach farmer Don Walters, for Colonel Ed Fletcher and for Douglas Fairbanks, Sr., irrigating acres and acres of orange groves at Fairbank's Ranch."

The Arballos, along with Aunt Seraphina who'd come along to housekeep, moved into one of five cottages that are still at the foot of 9th Street. Later Loreto bought the Alvarado House, built in 1884, on 10th street. This house, where Bill lived until he left for the army at seventeen, now sits on Del Mar's Fairgrounds, open to the public every July during the County Fair. "Restored to the way it looked in the 1880s," Bill said.

Going to Del Mar's two-room, two teacher, elementary school (where the Civic Center is now) was a great experience, Bill remembered. "The principal, Ruth Neimann, taught 4th to 8th grades, so if you were a 4th grader and finished your work early, you could learn by listening to her teaching the older kids."

At school there were rich kids and poor kids but no class, or race, discrimination, he said. "Although there was a "Caucasians Only" sign on Del

Mar's pier. The first time I noticed it I was nine, and going fishing. I thought a Caucasian was probably some kind of shellfish--like a clam."

Del Mar children of Bill's generation nearly always worked before school, and often afterwards, too. In Mrs. Neimann's class the snores of a weary boy named Christenson drifted regularly from the back of the room. The Arbello children tumbled out of bed about 4:30 a.m. to deliver both newspapers and milk.

"With so few people in town they needed us for a labor pool," Bill said. "When the tide flooded actor Pat O'Brian's beach house, as soon as the water receded, all the school children were rounded up to pack sandbags around the place."

"And every kid I knew worked at the drug store at some point. There were no rules about child labor, or alcohol and minors. The drug store sold liquor, and there was a special stool to stand on in case you were too short to reach it."

By fifteen he was driving boxes of alcohol from the drug store up the hill to the building on Avenida Primavera known as The Castle. "Which was a gambling den at the time," he said.

Del Mar's teenagers went to high school in Encinitas, at San Dieguito. To get there they caught the Greyhound bus outside the drug store, and then waited for the school bus in Encinitas outside Sturdevan's Drugs on the corner of 101 and G.

"We had a math teacher we all loved, Mrs. Brass, who was a terrible driver," Bill said. "Mrs. Brass would come steaming around the corner in her blue Chevrolet, papers flying around the back seat. We hid if we saw her coming. If she saw you first she'd put her head out of the window and call," Let me give you a lift!"

Cars, or rather the lack of them, played a large part in Bill's high school years.

"The boys hung out more in groups than gangs, " he said. "There were the Macnasties, who were sort of upper class. They had their own cars. I belonged to The Rowdies. We had one car between us, a 1929 Whippet."

Each Rowdie had the Whippet, an open sports car, for one day a week, Bill said. "My brother Bobby got it on Fridays--when it had flat tires, no gas and the water pump usually leaked."

It was, he said, "A great time to grow up. A big difference between then and today is there were fewer rules and regulations then. A building that would take years now would go up in months."

"My father could take a sack of peas he'd grown down to Miller's Grocery to barter, and nobody worried about those peas having been government inspected."

CHAPTER TWENTY SEVEN

The Rupe Family, Weathering Ups & Downs in early Encinitas"

Written May 1999

Next time you're passing the 7-11 in downtown Encinitas, on the corner of South Coast Highway 101 and D Street, you might find it fun to imagine yourself whisked back in time to 1915.

Blink a couple of times:

A horse-drawn wagon rumbles past you. The street is unpaved, dusty, edged with Eucalyptus trees. The 7-11 has vanished. In its place is J.W. Rupe's General Merchandise. Two horses hitched to a wooden railing slurp thirstily from a water trough and, towering beside the trough, is a bleached-white bone.

"It came from a whale that washed up on the beach," said Irene Rupe Swoboda, who was six in 1915 when her parents opened the store. It carried everything from wooden barrels of sugar to needles and dress fabrics. "It had a meat counter, a lunch counter and a pool hall," Irene remembers.

Occasionally, it also had colorfully-dressed gypsies, who worked in pairs.

"One would try to distract you, while the other one stole," Irene remembers. "Alice Lux, who worked in the store, would run and lock the door when she saw gypsies coming."

Irene and her older sister, Isabell, helped out after school and, when the store was quiet, practiced their pool shots.

"Sometimes men who came in would challenge us to a game," she says. "Their eyes would take in our satin hair ribbons, the ruffled dresses Mother sewed for us. We knew they were thinking, 'Those little girls can't possibly beat me.' But we did win, sometimes."

James, "J.W.", and Josephine Rupe were both born in Missouri and arrived in Encinitas in 1913. They first rented Peter Lux's house (still there) at 238 D Street. There were no other houses all the way to C Street, and the family had what Irene calls "a regular farm," with chickens, a milk cow, mules, horses and a pig. When Irene was twelve they moved to the Derby house, which stood all by itself by on a dusty trail that, today, is Vulcan Avenue.

"It had bathrooms! A big one and a small one. It was thrilling!" she said. "On D Street we'd been hauling water up in buckets from a well, and had to take baths in a copper tub in the kitchen."

The Derby House, built in the 1880s and privately owned now, had been a hotel, catering to passengers from the nearby train station. "The combined dining and living room ran the length of the building," Irene recalls. "And the built-in cabinets were beautiful, hand-crafted by Edward Hammond, who built the town's first schoolhouse."

All this glory cost $15 a month; the rent charged by the owner, a Methodist minister named Fay.

But the best thing about that year for the Rupe family was that Josephine, after twelve years, was expecting another baby.

"Father loved Isabell and me, but he wanted a son this time," Irene remembers. "When Faye--named after the kindly landlord--was born he was so disappointed he wouldn't look at her. One sunny morning Mother was sitting at the breakfast table with Faye on her lap. Father glanced over, and the baby smiled at him. For the rest of his life he adored her."

J.W. was a man with big dreams for a newer, better store. In 1928 he bought land on the corner of 2nd and D, and hired builder Miles Kellogg-- best-remembered, for his "Boat Houses" on 3rd Street. While the new store was being built Irene, now nineteen, was hired by the newly opened La Paloma Theater.

"I took tickets, and did the bookkeeping," she remembers. "But the best part of the job was that the theater had live Vaudedeville acts. It was my job to pay the performers, so every Saturday night I got to go down to their dressing rooms, under the stage, and meet them."

The new store that Miles Kellogg built for J.W. was, in the style of the '20s, art deco and stark white. It was actually four stores. (And still is, with Eagle Travel on the corner.).

"Father had such high hopes for it," Irene said. "But he soon realized he'd lost the "walk past" trade of First Street. And, within a year, the Great Depression began. Many of our customers, who'd run up large credit bills, didn't have the money to pay them."

In 1932, when a store from the big Safeway Stores Inc. chain opened on First Street, it was the final blow. J.W. Rupe's General Merchandise folded.

"It nearly broke Father's heart to lose both his building and his business," Irene said. "But he forged on. He went back to painting, which he'd done before, and, for years, worked steadily painting the Del Mar fairgrounds."

An interesting fact about her father, Irene said, is that although he moved to many different houses in this area he always rented them.

"In his eighty three years he never bought a house. His one venture into owning property was the land on which he built his dream store."

CHAPTER TWENTY EIGHT

"The King's Men"

Written February 2000

1961

At 8:30 on a summer evening 21-year-old Warren Raps waited anxiously outside Chuck's Sportsman's Top Shop, on 101, on the south edge of Encinitas.

Warren had spent the past half hour inside Chuck's, trying to convince the members of The King's Men Car Club they should vote him in. This wasn't an easy club to join. As well as having a good driving record, no jail-time, a respectable job and a car they could race, prospective King's Men had to make a speech containing the "magic phrase."

Warren glanced down at his watch. 8:35...8:36...Time seemed to be crawling. Had his speech been okay? Would the other members vote him in?

He had never wanted anything so much in his life.

The Raps family, consisting of Warren, his father, mother, grandmother, sister Maxine and their German Sheppard, moved to Cardiff in 1956; to a house on the corner of Mozart and San Elijo.

"The only problem with Cardiff was there were no sewers then, and we didn't know much about septic tanks," Warren remembers. "Each time ours overflowed a guy driving a tank truck called " the honey wagon" would come and pump it out. While he pumped he used to sit there reading the Old Testament."

For teenaged boys in the late '50s, owning an auto was almost as important as breathing. Warren's first car, bought mainly with lawn-mowing and avocado-picking money, was a 1939 Ford sedan in dire need of work.

"My dad, a master mechanic in the aerospace industry, loved working on cars. Fixing that sedan together was no problem," Warren said. "But he wouldn't let me drive it until I'd paid for a year's insurance. That cost $45. It was back to the lawn-mowing."

By the time he applied to join The King's Men, Warren was working full time--for landscape contractor Carl Sneider--and his car was a brand new convertible. A Ford Starliner; it had white-walled tires, fins, and chrome practically everywhere.

By 8:45 p.m. on that night in 1961, Warren was still standing on the highway, staring at the closed door of Chuck's Sportman's Top Shop. His best buddy, Walter Drew, who was five years older than he was and a typesetter at The Coast Dispatch newspaper, belonged to The King's Men. It was Walt who'd taught him the magic phrase. Walt won more races than anybody in the club, but he was battling muscular dystrophy. Sometimes, to change gears, he had to fling his body across the seat.

The King's Men wore purple jackets, like letterman's jackets, embroidered on the back with a drunken horse carrying a knight waving a rod and piston. At races club members watched out for each other, making sure no one cheated; even if that meant they had to pay a $75 dismantling fee to check out a competitor's engine. In a way the King's Men were like musketeers; one for all and all for one.

Warren was thinking about this when Walt came out and said, "You're in!"

Until 1964, when Carlsbad's Raceway opened on Palomar Road, local car clubs often drag-raced, two cars at a time, at an abandoned airstrip near Paradise Mesa. No prize money then, just trophies. "You got a yellow sticker every time you won, so Walt's car's was blanketed in yellow," Warren remembers. "He'd taunt the guy behind him, waving his arm, yelling, 'Come on!'"

The King's Men were known as the Solana Beach King's Men, even thought they met in Encinitas. At the time Warren joined members included a mortician, a plumber, the owner of a service station, a carpenter and a dental technician. All of them were young. If you'd seen them hanging out at an Encinitas drive-in on Highway 101 called The Dump (now the upscale restaurant "When In Rome") with their slicked-back hair, arms folded, leaning back against their souped-up cars, you might have thought them a wild bunch.

"Not so," Warren said. "The King's Men had strict rules about road conduct, and anyone who broke them went before a kangaroo court." The club, he said, started the designated sober driver at parties long before that phrase went into the language. They assisted stranded motorists, and "adopted" San Diego's Sunshine School for children with physical challenges, donating money and working on the school's buildings.

For a couple of years they had a float in the Encinitas Christmas Parade.

"Regis Philbin was Master of Ceremonies one of those years," Warren remembers. "It poured with rain, really thundered down, and Regis drove down in a convertible. Next day I heard him say on television that driving into Encinitas was like, "Driving into the valley of doom."

By the late '60s the draft, marriage and the expense of raising children had whittled down the club's membership, and eventually they disbanded. But Warren, who stayed a bachelor, still races and is a mechanic for his two nephews who often race in Carlsbad.

"We used to start in a blaze of smoke and screaming rubber," he said "The first day I reached 130 m.p.h. I thought I was really hot stuff. Now they're going 300 m.p.h."

CHAPTER TWENTY NINE

"Drugstore Soda Fountains Once Gathering Places"

Written January 2001

    Some people believe it's a myth, but I've always loved the story of Lana Turner being discovered perched on a soda fountain stool at Schwab's Drugstore. (She was playing hooky from Hollywood High, while wearing a tight Angora sweater.)

Being in a drugstore in the late '30s, early '40s, was to be in a different world from the Wal-Mart lookalikes of today.

"The soda fountain's counter was a gathering place," says Janet Knipe Bertoncini who in her teens worked at Luttrell's, an Encinitas drugstore on the corner of E and Coast Highway 101. (It was a few doors south of the three buildings recently destroyed by fire.) The same customers usually turned up daily, she said, including her boy-friend, Ernie, who liked malts so thick a spoon stood upright in them. Patients of Dr. Novak, whose surgery was across the street, knew if they needed to find him at lunchtime, he'd be on a stool at the fountain, munching a grilled cheese sandwich.

"The Greyhound bus stopped right outside. As well as selling tickets we put packages on the bus, and the driver dropped packages off," Janet said. "One day the driver handed me a package on which I noticed the words 'Remains of....'."

She realized, she said, that someone's ashes had just come in on the bus. "And I'd known the guy! It was a very strange feeling."

"I think every kid in town worked in the Del Mar Drug Store at some point," Bill Arballo said, adding that sixty years ago the entire population of Del Mar numbered about three hundred. Bill, who got twenty cents an hour--"and all the ice cream I could eat"--said no one worried about age restrictions. "Kids of nine, ten, worked there. Harry Johnson, the druggist, kept a box behind the counter for kids too short to reach the cash register."

Those who couldn't reach the highest shelves also clambered on the box to get liquor bottles down for customers, Bill said. "We knew what everybody in town was drinking. Including Ten High, the cheapest form of bourbon that would give you a terrible headache."

Like Luttrell's, the soda fountain counter in Del Mar was a sociable place. Bill recalls a day when Bing Crosby came in with the local plumber, Ed Dunham.

"They'd been fishing, and had cleaned their fish before they came in. As they sat at the counter the two of them smelled pretty bad," he said.

"A woman who was sitting near Bing and Ed complained. She told Harry Johnson, 'If you don't throw those bums out, I'll never come in here again!' But when it was explained to her that she was complaining about Bing Crosby she asked him for his autograph."

Solana Beach's drugstore was on 101, a block south of the Plaza. In 1934, when Jim King was eight, he had a job sweeping the sidewalk outside. "You never heard of a kid getting pocket money back then," he said. "So we'd all go around the merchants asking if they'd anything we could do." Every Thursday Jim delivered the Saturday Evening Post around town--"It cost a nickel, and I got to keep one cent,"--and then he'd stand outside the drugstore trying to sell his leftover copies. "Mr. Kurtz, the druggist, put a stop to that because he was selling the Post inside," Jim remembers. "The ones with Norman Rockwell covers always sold best."

By 1943, when three 15-year-old school friends--Lauralie Dunn, Virginia Wilkens and Joyce Mckenna--worked at Solana Beach's drug store fountain it had become Dietrich's Drugs. The place was usually packed, Lauralie remembers.

"During the war people didn't have the gasoline to go far from home," she said. "and we got a lot of hitchhiking servicemen." One Sunday, Lauralie and Mr. Dietrich were the only ones there when several buses pulled up outside. "150 service men, having a day off, were heading for the beach," Lauralie said. "And the drug store was the only place they could find food and drink!."

In those days cokes didn't come in bottles, but were actually assembled at the fountain, a process involving a lot of squirting from pumps.

"First you took a narrow-bottomed coke glass and covered the bottom with crushed ice," Lauralie said. "Then you squirted in the coke syrup." The next step, she explained, was squirting in carbonated water followed by the grand finale, the flavoring. "Most people asked for lemon or cherry cokes, but some of the wilder ones liked the chocolate we used on sundaes."

Unfortunately, nobody remembers seeing Lana Turner sipping any kind of coke at a local fountain. But Janet Knipes Bertoncini remembers that her biggest tip came from two movie stars.

It was the early '40s, by which time Janet had married Ernie Bertoncini, the boy-friend who loved the malts she made at Luttrell's.

"Ernie's brother, Bob, had a small cafe in Del Mar, called the Bob In," she said. "It was on 15th Street." (Del Mar's drug store was on the corner of 15th and 101, and both it and the Bob In were across the street from the Del Mar Hotel, now L'Auberge.).

She was helping out at the Bob In, Janet remembers, when Tony Martin and Rita Hayworth walked in.

"They were both so nice. They were on their way to the beach and asked if I'd put coffee in a thermos they had with them," Janet said. "For doing this they tipped me a dollar. To me it was like getting a million!"

CHAPTER THIRTY

"Pines, Spaghetti and Puddles Part of Cardiff School's History"

Written February 2000

    My husband, Scotty, who faithfully swallows Ginko Biloba every morning as a memory aid, remembers vividly that when our kids were going to Cardiff Elementary School, both principals there could remember every child's name.

This was in the years from the 1960s to the '80s. There was Ed Kufahl, (who did everything, including shepherding kids across the street). Ed was followed by George Berkich, who, like Dick Clark, never seemed to age, and was so progressive he went surfing with his students.

Apparently this 87-year-old school (first built in 1913, and rebuilt in 1950) was always a spirited place. Even in the Depression, the three teachers--Principal Miss Domenigoni, Miss Jorgensen and Mrs. Pullman--managed to provide shade for the playground by offering to plant a tree for any child who could bring in fifty cents.

"Our mothers used to come in and cook lunch," Jay Harold Williams remembers of those Depression years. Meat in a school lunch was almost unheard of then, he said. "Sometimes it was just beans. There was a basement downstairs, and there must have been a stove there because I know when it was my mother's turn she didn't cook the lunch at home. Children paid a nickel if they could, but some of the new children in Cardiff were living with their families in garages, coming to school barefoot."

The school was still in the original wooden building, then, named The Cullen School because Cardiff's founder, J. Frank Cullen, donated the land. There were only three classrooms, shared by eight grades.

"We had about forty students. And one of the grades had five girls called 'Barbara'," remembers Mary Ann Wiegand Wood.

Some lunches may have been "just beans", but never on Wednesdays. Wednesdays were wonderful because George Beech, who owned George's, a restaurant in Cardiff down on the beach, (a famous place, where movie stars often ate), donated lunch to the school every Wednesday.

"He'd arrive with big trays of things like spaghetti," Herb Lux remembers.

Herb's favorite teacher was lovely Miss Jorgenson, who wore T-strap shoes and swooped her hair into waves with a Marcel waving iron. It was Miss Jorghansen who, when he was six, taught Herb's class how to use the telephone.

"My parents had just got one, but very few homes in the area had a telephone then," Herb said. "Our number was 46."

"When Miss Jorgensen cranked up the handle and handed me the bone-shaped receiver a strange lady's voice came floating through it. She kept saying, over and over, 'Your Number, please?' I panicked and shouted 'I want to talk to my mom!'"

With no school bus, and a "scrape the barrel" budget, field trips were rare. Most class outings consisted of rushing outside the classroom whenever something interesting was happening in Cardiff.

The event of the new Streamline train passing through on its way to the San Diego World's fair was definitely interesting. "It was the first one we'd seen that wasn't a steam train," Herb said. "It didn't stop in Cardiff. But we all walked to the bluffs across from the school and lined up, waving, beside the tracks."

Low-flying air ships, known as dirigibles, were another reason to rush outside as they glided majestically over Cardiff on their way to Camp Kearney. "They were huge. About eight hundred feet long," Herb remembers. "You could always hear them coming--a unique sound, like a deep, baritone groan."

Now, nearly a century after the first Cardiff teacher, Eve Eckerson, taught for $675 a year, the current school is on the verge of being radically modernized. (If residents approve a bond issue on March 7th.) If you began your education there in the Kufahl or Berkich eras, or, like me, had children who did, you may be feeling relieved that, whatever happens, that building, with all its memories, isn't going to be totally demolished.

Do you remember "Hobo Days" when the kids spent recess digging holes in an adjacent field so they could cook like hobos? Or how Alta Nelson's third graders planted a tree in the school grounds every Arbor Day?

"Before he gave the Torrey Pines seedlings to us, Herb Lux always grew them to about the same height as the third graders," Alta remembers. "So we nicknamed him Cardiff's Johnny Appleseed."

Perhaps you remember Audrey Fixen, the red-haired cafeteria manager who convinced kids washing dishes was fun? (Mrs. Fixen's sideline was income tax preparation, but I used to think she must be a hypnotist, too.)

Can you remember Cardiff School's famous puddles?

Every rainy season enormous puddles formed in the corners of the playground, and spread under the chain link fence into San Elijo Avenue. The kids used to flatten their bodies against the fence waiting for a car to speed by and drench them with sprayed puddle water.

It's always been a spirited place.

CHAPTER THIRTY ONE

" Terrace Rats Stick With Traditional Tattoo"

Written June 1999

    The original Terrace Rats were a dozen boys who had grown up together in Del Mar Terrace, and formed a gang. This was around 1950, when they were eleven or twelve.

"We were never a 'gang' gang, like the Los Angeles' Bloods and Crips," said Joe Gooding, ("Big Joe" to his friends.) "Mostly we roamed the area--hunting, fishing, looking for adventures."

Climbing to the sandstone rock named The Donut, because it had a big hole in the middle, definitely qualified as an adventure. The Donut (gone now, blasted down by a developer) extended out from a high cliff and was so dangerous to reach that many parents forbade their kids to tackle it. Anxious Terrace mothers used to watch The Donut from their kitchen windows with binoculars.

As Joe talked during a recent interview I kept seeing both the Rats, and his own family, in a series of images, like film clips.

Click: There's Joe's dad, James W. Gooding, the first person in the North County to service refrigerators, rattling around in his truck with "There Goes Jimmy the Fixit" on the back.

Click: Joe's dad again, hunkered down tossing dice in the street outside Eden Garden's Blue Bird Cafe.

(Enjoying gambling was only one side of Jimmy the Fixit. He was a Kiwanis president, a Scout leader and built the Terrace's community meeting hall in his spare time.)

Click click: There's Joe's beautiful older sister, Kay, Miss San Dieguito in 1955, tattooing "TRS" above her brother's left ankle.

"Without the tattoo you couldn't be a true member of the gang," Joe explained.

Today's Del Mar Terrace area, which includes Del Mar Heights, conjures up words like "affluent" and "upscale". Back in 1942, when James and Velva Gooding moved there with their four children, it was a country area--bean fields, rutted tracks, lots of horses, backed by the beauty of the mountains.

When Joe started at Soledad school (closed in 1948 because its bathrooms were outhouses) he rode there on his horse, Trigger. Typical of this warm, close-knit community was that farmer Frank Knechtel donated a cow every year for a deep-pit barbecue.

"Everyone knew everyone," Joe said. "There were only three houses on our street, plus Mrs. Elm's chicken ranch."

Joe was the Goodings' youngest child, four years old when they moved in.

To call his childhood eventful seems a bit of an understatement. Within a few years after arriving in The Terrace he'd managed to crush his upper left arm in his mother's laundry mangle. (The only doctor available was also a vet, who rubbed on horse liniment that took off all the skin).

He also broke both wrists falling into a canyon from a one-rope swing, rescued a 67-year-old man from drowning and, of course, joined the gang.

"Some guys got the tattoo on the shoulder, I wanted it where my parents wouldn't see it," he said. So Kay, fourteen then, took him to her boyfriend's home in Eden Gardens.

"She dipped a needle in Indian ink and jabbed it through cotton, "Joe remembers. He also remembers it hurt like hell, but, hey, to be a Terrace Rat you couldn't be wimpy about such things.

The gang had several pairs of close-in-age brothers, including the Skinners, Bob and Gene, the Pollorenos, Eddie and Larry, and Jimmy and John Love Smith. "John had a hard time when he grew older," Joe said. "No one believed he was really a John Smith."

Click: Another image. There's Camp Callan Army base, at Torrey Pines. The Terrace Rats are scrambling around two huge, 150-gun landing craft once used for practicing landing on enemy beaches. The friendly guy managing the mess hall gives them war-vintage Twinkies, without realizing the cakes are now filled with cobwebs.

By the late '50s, the original kids had, naturally, outgrown the gang. But Joe--who at twenty wore his hair in a pompadour and had won an Elvis look-alike contest--became a mentor to a new bunch of Rats. A kind of "King Rat". He used to take them surf fishing, and teach them bicycle repair.

By 1970, he said, there were Rats who were sons of the original gang, including his own son, Jimmy Joe.

I asked Joe if, with all the new buildings, the great swoops of freeway, there were any Terrace rats still roaming around.

In 1994, he said, he stopped in at Del Mar's U-Totem market. "I was on my way back from fishing in Ensenada, and four or five boys hanging around the parking lot were curious about the yellow tail and rock cod in the back of my truck. As one kid leaned forward, his T-shirt sleeve hiked up, showing TRS."

Joe rolled up his pants leg and showed the boys his faded-to-blue tattoo. "First generation, guys," he said.

They all stared at him. "Wow!' one of them said finally. "We've heard stories......"

And then, right there in the parking lot, Joe said, they raised their arms and bowed to him.

CHAPTER THIRTY TWO

"A Fascination With the Past Leads Cardiff Couple into Adventures"

Written June 1998

The words "This is a first" kept leaping into my mind when I went to see the friendly, antique-collecting Youngs--Dave and Bertha--in their home on Crest Drive, which is Cardiff's highest point.

It was the first time I'd been in a house that was built around the original home of one of Cardiff's earliest settlers. The settler was Walter Mackinnon (whose brother, Hector, arrived here ahead of everybody, except the Indians, in 1875.)

A copy of the deeds to the property, signed in 1895, hangs beside the Young's front door. There's also a photo of Walter--looking very much the grizzled prospector with his raggedy white beard and suspenders--standing outside a copper mine that once existed at the end of Olivenhain's Lone Jack Road.

Another "first" moment happened when I saw the Young's living room. Glass-fronted cases holding hundreds of things people used to use in their everyday lives, range in front of the floor to ceiling windows. Larger wooden pieces that Dave mended and restored himself--like the yarn-winder from the mid 1800s, the spinning wheel picked up at an auction--loom in each direction you turn.

"Is it...like living in a museum?" I asked Bertha, who smiled and said that she didn't set out to collect, but one thing lead to another. Her collection of flat irons, for example. It began with one Dave's mother used in the '30s, and has multiplied to about 60, including a 98-year-old electric tea iron used for both ironing and boiling water for tea.

"When we travel we stay off the freeways," Bertha said. "We love going to yard sales, and those stores that have "Antiques" up on a sign. But you know it's going to be mostly really good junk. We don't spend a lot, but sometimes, when we get home and start researching, we'll find something's quite valuable. It adds to the fun."

Dave's mother, Azalea Young, who taught school in Encinitas, at Central, in the '30s, 40s and '50s, contributed some of the antiques. The Indian wedding ceremonial vase--with a spout on each side for the couple to drink from --was one she found while teaching on the Pala reservation in the '20s.

"She liked designing houses," Dave said of his mother, who was widowed while still in her thirties. "When we moved to Leucadia, in 1932, she designed our house on Eoleus." Money was tight, he remembers. The house was single-walled, with tongue-in-groove knotty pine; no studs. "Whenever there was a strong wind the walls rippled."

Bertha Young is a quilter, and in the house on Crest Drive her sewing room holds fifteen antique sewing machines (including a "Singer" that once sailed around The Horn with its emigrating German owners).

Soon after she met Dave, twenty-four years ago, their shared love of the past was obvious. They were driving back from a Christmas trip to Montana (her home state)when they discovered the oak, 1902, hand-operated wooden washing machine, with mangle, that now stands in their kitchen. "Dave had to take it apart to fit it into the trunk and back seat of his Mercedes sedan. He kidded me that, 'If anything has to go on the roof it'll be you,'" Bertha said, laughing.

The kitchen is filled with as many intriguing antiques as the rest of the house. Above the back door (the same door Walter Mackinnon used in 1895) a wooden sign states simply "Bessie B". Dave discovered it in the original stables, leading them to wonder if perhaps Mackinnon named his horses Bessie A, B, and C, etc.

The Young's back yard is the most unusual part of their property. A place of natural beauty--their two and three quarter acres includes the canyon wall that swoops craggily down to where Herb Lux's farmland borders the Greek Church--Dave has reconstructed a saloon of the "Gunsmoke" kind there, using wood from a bunk house bulldozed at Meadowlark Ranch. There's a blacksmith's forge there, too; and a store with the counter from Eden's Garden's first grocery store. The horse-drawn wagon that once delivered water to this area's early settlers rests near the canyon's rim.

"Right now we're storing things for the Heritage Museum," Dave said. "When the new Heritage Park gets built, on the corner of Vulcan and Encinitas Boulevard, I'll be moving a lot of this stuff over there."

A final "This is definitely a first" moment happened as I was leaving the Youngs, and spotted the antique pig-oiler on their doorstep. Dave explained that if a pig rubbed against this square metal object, with its two wheels and a hole for pouring in oil, the animal would automatically get lubricated. Pigs, apparently, need this as they've no sweat glands, and their skin is inclined to be sensitive. On the path beside the doorstep I noticed several concrete pigs "slumbering" in the sunshine.

"Our grown children gave us those when they found out we had a pig-oiler," Bertha said." One thing just keeps on leading to another."

CHAPTER THIRTY THREE

"Lyle Hammond, the Irresistible Eagle Beak"

Written June 1999

Last April I mentioned that although I'd never met Lyle Hammond--who was born in Leucadia in 1893, and died in 1979--I keep meeting women who describe him as irresistible. It might have been forty, or fifty years since they last saw him but, at the mere mention of his name, a certain light flickers into their eyes.

One particularly vivacious woman, Joan Weir Dayton, who I met in the Heritage Museum, actually broke into song when I mentioned him.

Now, having spoken to dozens of people who knew him, I realize it wasn't only women who liked Lyle. Men did, children did, just about everyone did.

When I picture Lyle now, I see a cheerful man strumming a ukulele on Moonlight Beach as he sings, "Put your arms around me, honey."

"He had the kind of personality where people jumped at the chance to be with him," said his nephew, Bob Grice. "He was fun. And, even if you were a kid, he made you feel important."

But no one, Bob added, would describe Lyle as movie-star handsome. He was lean, wiry, with a wide smile, a prominent nose. The dance band he used to play in, The Encinitas Ranch Hands, nicknamed him "Eagle Beak".

Lyle, his brother Sam, and sister Janie were all born on their grandfather Edward Hammond's place, Sunset Ranch. The ranch stood all by itself, where, today, Leucadia Boulevard runs into the golf course. In the '30s, when their father, Ted Hammond, died, and their mother, Mary, moved from the ranch down to C Street in Encinitas, the family joked that she was, "moving to the big city."

The Hammonds were a musically gifted family. Sunset Ranch was famous locally for evenings where, as well as classical music, everyone gathered around the piano to sing. Lyle favored the romantic songs, like "I Wonder Who's Kissing Her Now?"

"I can still hear him singing," said Lyle's niece, Bettie Wolfe, who, fifty years ago, fox-trotted and jitterbugged with him across the shiny-as-glass wooden floor of Carlsbad's Twin Inns. (Now Neimans).

After fighting in France in the first World War, and driving a school bus, Lyle spent over thirty years working in Encinitas Post office. He lived in an apartment in the courtyard beside the La Paloma theater, and later in a house on A Street, and got married three times--to Francis, Erma and Vickie.

"He always had had a great deal of energy," said Bob Grice, who remembers driving around dark, country roads with Lyle, around four in the morning, on Lyle's moonlighting job delivering the Los Angeles Examiner.

"When the dawn came up we'd go swimming on Moonlight Beach, and then Lyle would go in to work at the post office."

Like his nose, Lyle's La Paloma apartment had a nickname. Actually it had two, "The Casino" and "Grand Central Station."

"Because it was always open-house there," remembers Betty Jo Swaim, who was one of a group of teenagers Lyle allowed to party in his apartment in the early '40s."We called him 'Pops', and we all loved him."

The parties, Betty Jo says, were never the wild kind----"Mostly dancing and singing"--although they did once spike Lyle's water cooler with gin.

"He never locked his door. One morning I dropped by and there was a sailor asleep on the couch. He'd just wandered in off the street and gone to sleep. Lyle said he'd assumed he was left over from the previous night's party."

Lyle's daughter, Jean, and son, Jerry, lived with him in "Grand Central Station" until the war, when Jerry went off to the South Pacific with the Navy.

"In those days the post office was the center of Encinitas," Jerry Hammond remembers. "Everyone had to go there." During the war, he said, his friendly, easy-going father always wrote something encouraging on the backs of letters going to servicemen. "So, on many of the letters coming into the post office there'd be a message to Dad on the envelope."

When Jerry was on the USS Oceanus in the South Pacific, he said, his father mailed him every edition of the local newspaper. "Filled with ordinary, everyday news of North County people," he said. "The entire ship read them, and I'd get them back in tatters."

Towards the end of his life arthritis prevented Lyle from driving, but it didn't slow down his charm, or ability to have fun.

"His third wife, Vickie, was blind in one eye," Bob Grice remembers. "But not long before he died she drove them all the way to Alaska in a camper to which she'd attached the bumper sticker "Jesus is our Wagon Master".

Lyle's memorial service was held at the Encinitas Legion hall, on 3rd Street. Vickie sat down at the piano and launched into some of Lyle's favorite songs, including "When the Midnight Choo Choo leaves For Alabam."

"And that's the way Lyle went out," said Bettie Jo Swaim. "With Vickie banging away at that piano and all of us singing the old songs."

CHAPTER THIRTY FOUR

"Using Up the Leftovers"

Written October 1998

My thrifty Scottish mother-in-law used up her leftovers by flinging them into an iron pot. She kept it simmering on the stove, and over several days a piece of sausage might be joined by a blob of mashed potato, a cupful of oxtail soup, a scrap of bacon rind. Somehow it all melded together into an interesting stew.

Once, when I was visiting her in Dundee Scotland, I left a poached egg uneaten on my plate at breakfast. With a cry of , "You're no going to waste that, are ye?" Ma tossed the egg into the iron pot.

This week's column reminds me of that pot. I'm using up half a dozen stories "left over" from column interviews. Reba Brereton's story of being born during the 1918 flu epidemic, for instance.

Reba has lived in the same house in Leucadia since 1948, but she was born in a small town in the foothills of the Ozark Mountains.

"Our telephone was on a party line, so when my father tried to call the doctor other voices joined in," she told me. "I've just seen Dr. Throgmartin's car turning into the Clutter's driveway,' someone told him. 'Try there.'"

Dr. Throgmartin wasn't at the Clutter's, so Reba's father dashed back to his wife and told her to hold on. Then he dashed back to the phone, and another disembodied voice chimed in with, "'I've just seen the doctor going towards the Jessup's place."

"The doctor was so busy that night, going from flu victim to flu victim, that he never did make it to our place," Reba said. "Finally my father delivered me himself. He was a farmer, and was used to delivering cows, but I'm sure my mother would have rather had Dr. Throgmartin!"

A few weeks ago, when I wrote about Dr. Lindsay's wife, a tall, strong nurse affectionately known as "Enema Mary", I was short of space and had to leave out her lemonade story.

"When my father came back from World War II he set up his medical practice in our Encinitas home," the Lindsays' daughter, Elaine Harris, told me." My mother was able to use her favorite treatment for anyone who came in drunk-- which was to put them in a fiercely hot bath, and make them drink glass after glass of lemonade." (There's a rumor among longtime residents that one man actually climbed out of a window to avoid this treatment.)

If you moved here after the North County began to be built up you've probably never found a rattlesnake curled under your kitchen stove; but earlier residents had many experiences with them.

In the column about Bob Grice's boyhood, on the Sunset Ranch in 1930s Leucadia, I described him wandering the hills when he was ten, a forked stick in one hand, a sack in the other, hunting rattlesnakes. That was only half the story, though. The untold part is that it was amazing that Bob's mother, Janie Hammond Grice, agreed to let him do this. She'd been almost killed by a rattlesnake bite, in 1901, when she was three.

"She was playing outside Sunset Ranch, when a snake slithered across the ground in front of her," Bob told me. "She'd once seen her father kill a rattler with a rock, so she picked up a stone and tried to do the same thing."

The snake moved more quickly than Janie did.

In 1901 the nearest doctor was in Escondido. By the time Janie's frantic parents had driven from Leucadia to Escondidio, in a horse drawn buggy over rough roads, the little girl's arm was black, and hugely swollen." For the rest of her life," Bob said, "She had a scar near her wrist as large as my watchband."

It was also Bob Grice who told me, after I'd written a column mentioning wartime beer rationing at Miller's Grocery Store, about Sam Miller's dramatic book-burning party.

"Many people who lived around here in the '30s didn't have enough money to feed their families during the Depression," Bob told me. "Sam carried them, letting them charge their groceries." Sam, whose store was on Highway 101 and the corner of E Street, on the side where the railroad tracks are, recorded what was owed in small, fifty page "tab books", using a different book for each family.

"He had a whole rack of those books, " Bob said."And twenty years later, when he retired, he still had a whole rack of them. He told everyone who owed him money that they no longer owed him a thing. On his last day of business Sam

Miller walked out into the alley behind his store, lit a bonfire, and tossed in the tab books. He burnt the lot."

Food stories, of course, frequently crop up when you're talking about the past. One warm September afternoon Marguerite Miller, (no relation to Sam), and I were chatting casually in the back room of San Dieguito's Heritage Museum. She told me that her father, Alwin Wiegand, who was born near Olivenhain in 1887, hated to see anyone at his table eat their dessert first.

"My mother, Frieda, was a wonderful cook, so they were always able to keep very good workers on their farm," Marguerite said. "My father didn't mind how much any of them ate. But I once saw him almost fire a farmhand because the man spread jam on a piece of bread at the start of the meal, before he'd eaten his meat and vegetables."

I left the museum thinking that I'd love to use the bread and jam story. But where? In which column? Then I realized something, like that blob of mashed potato Ma once tossed into her iron pot, Marguerite's story was a usable leftover. In fact, I had lots of usable leftovers. If I tossed some into a column they might, with a bit of luck, meld together into an interesting stew.

CHAPTER THIRTY FIVE

"Movie Stars Most Visible in Old Del Mar"

Written September 2000

    My relatives were extremely disappointed in me the first time I returned from Cardiff-By-The-Sea to Manchester, England. Not only was I the same boring shade of pale pink as when I had left--English people believe all residents of Southern California have spectacular tans--I hadn't brought back any stories about local encounters with movie stars.

"But you've been there three years!" my Auntie Peggy said. "You must have met movie stars."

This was back in the '60s, and I'm smarter now. On my annual trips to Britain I go prepared with stories about local encounters with stars. True, they're rarely my own encounters; but my relatives don't really care as long as I'm entertaining them over scones and tea. (Or sherry, in the case of the wilder ones.)

Sharon Seebert Strand told me the story of Bette Davis' skirt. In the '30s Sharon's father, Lloyd "Bert" Seebert managed the Inn at Rancho Santa Fe.

"Bette Davis was staying there, and planned to wear a tight-fitting, white sharkskin suit to the Del Mar races," Sharon said. "She sent the suit to the hotel laundry to be pressed."

Apparently whoever pressed it felt nervous about touching a hot iron to white sharkskin. "So they covered it with newspaper," Sharon said. "And the print came off on the skirt. Bette was furious. But she wore it to the races anyway, and strode around with newsprint on her rear view."

If you lived in Del Mar in the years immediately before and after World War II it wasn't unusual, because of the race track, to find yourself standing beside stars like Gregory Peck and Betty Grable in the drug store.

"The town was so small then movie stars were very visible," Don Terwilliger said. "There was really only one place they could stay, the Del Mar Hotel."

Don's aunt, Del Mar's Postmaster Mae Kibbler--"She never used the term Postmistress," he said--lived at the hotel. So as a kid Don spent a great deal of time being starstruck in the lobby.

"A lot of famous couples stayed there," he recalled. "In May '49 Clark Gable came down with his wife at that time, Lady Sylvia Ashly, to watch a big car race at the track. It was a 100-mile race, so the cars raced around the track one hundred times."

It was also in '49, Don remembered, that Rita Hayworth--whose pin-up photograph in a satin nightgown was considered so hot GIs pasted it on the first atom bomb detonated at Bikini Atoll--stayed at Del Mar's Hotel with her horse-racing enthusiast husband, Prince Aly Khan.

One of this area's most frequently-encountered movie stars, because he lived in Rancho Santa Fe for years, was Victor Mature.

Lola Larsen, who lives in Leucadia, was around fourteen when her uncle, director Hal Roach, discovered Mature. He launched his career in the 1940's "One Million BC", where Mature got to race around in a brief loincloth battling warring tribes and historically-inaccurate dinosaurs. (The dinosaurs were actually magnified lizards.)

"I thought he was so gorgeous in that loincloth! I was smitten," Lola remembers. "My father was a terrible tease, and one day when we met Victor Mature on the studio lot I had to stand there cringing with embarrassment as Dad introduced me to him as "My daughter who thinks you look good without your clothes on."

The most unusual anecdote I've heard about Victor Mature came from one of the students in my MiraCosta writing classes, Cherie Emeno, whose father, Irv, played golf with Mature.

"He often came to Dad's house in Solana Beach," Cherie remembers. Mature enjoyed taking photographs, and he liked the people in them to be smiling, she said. " If they weren't smiling he'd quickly zip his pant's zipper up and down as he held the camera. It certainly worked on my grandfather. He was in his mid eighties, and feeling kind of sad that day, but in the after-zipper photograph he's laughing."

When I interviewed Ruth McKnight Eischen about the days when her husband, Les, managed Douglas Fairbanks, Sr.'s orange groves--now Fairbanks Ranch area--she mentioned how sad many people felt in the 1930s when Douglas left Mary Pickford and married the divorced wife of a British peer, Lady Sylvia Ashly. (It was after Fairbanks died that Lady Sylvia married Clark Gable. "She got around," Don Terwilliger said.)

"Years later Les and I were touring Carlsbad Caverns in New Mexico and I felt a tap on my shoulder," Ruth Eischen recalled. "It was Mary Pickford, with her second husband, actor Buddy Rodgers. I knew she'd remember Les, but I was amazed that she remembered me. She said she'd always loved the ranch, but Fairbanks had given her the choice of taking it or Pickfair, the mansion in Beverly Hills that he'd built for her in 1920 as a wedding present. Losing Pickfair would have meant losing her home."

Last July I almost had a celebrity encounter myself, on 2nd Street in Encinitas. I was in Dalager's sharpening store when Danny Dalager mentioned Grammy-award winning singer Patti Page was next-door, getting a manicure.

I did think of popping next-door for a chat, but didn't like to infringe on Patti's 's privacy. And this, probably, is why, on future trips to Britain, my relatives will still be hearing about other people's encounters with celebrities.

CHAPTER THIRTY SIX

"The Friendly Dalagers"

Written July 2000

If you happen to be driving along 2nd Street, in the old part of downtown Encinitas, as you pass Dalager's Sharpening Service, at 820, you'll be passing the site of one of the town's first buildings. The house known as Grandma Lux's House used to stand on that spot.

The Dalager family bought the house from Alice Lux Lamplugh in the '60s. In the '70s, while still living there, they tore down the old house, slowly, and built their shop there.

The tearing down process was full of surprises, Danny Dalager said, including finding nearly a hundred years worth of rat droppings. "They were piled up three-feet high behind one wall," he said. "We discovered that the wall boards were nailed to studs, only the studs weren't nailed to anything. In Encinitas in the 1890s they didn't need permits. There were so few people in town then the Lux family probably just got together and hammered it up themselves."

The Dalagers own history in Encinitas began during World War II when Hans E.O. Dalager, a Norwegian from South Dakota, met Valora Middleton, from Illinois. Both were in the Marine Corps at Camp Pendleton.

"We were married in 1946, at Cardiff's Little Chapel of the Roses, and then rented a cottage on Leucadia's Hygeia," Valora said.

Hans kept on working at Camp Pendleton in a Civil Service job, but in his spare time he opened a sharpening service in their landlord's former chicken coup.

"I think both the cottage and the chicken coup are still there, in the 800 block," Valora said. "A family named Blodgett lived there after we did. Until the day he died Mr. Blodgett used to tell me, every time we met, that he was the oldest surfer in town."

By 1953 the Dalager family had grown to six with the arrivals of Carol, Orville, Danny and Myron. Danny was born on the day, September 3rd 1950, that they moved to Cardiff-By-The-Sea.

"We moved into our house, on Manchester Avenue, in the morning," Valora said. "As Danny arrived in the afternoon I didn't get around to putting things away. The kids used to tease me that I never did get around to it."

Nearly all longtime Cardiffians remember Valora. Before working full-time at Cardiff post office, for about twenty five years, she delivered our mail as Phyllis Lux's substitute.

"In those days Cardiff didn't have a mail truck. We used our own cars," she said. "I remember one lady who used to call out to me 'Hi, Phyllis!' I think her eyesight wasn't good. One day I trotted up to her and said, 'I'm not Phyllis,' and she looked closely at me and exclaimed 'Oh, you're right, you're not!'"

In 1960 Hans retired from his Camp Pendleton job and moved his business --sharpening everything from lawn mowers to chain saws--to 2nd Street. Soon after that the family moved into Grandma Lux's house. It was during the big earthquake of 1968 that they realized, Danny said, how unstable their old house was.

"We ran out into the street and the whole house was creaking and swaying," he said.

In '76 Danny and Myron bought the sharpening business from their parents. Hans died in '92, and Valora now lives over the shop with Orville, who works for a flood control company.

"One by one the homes along 2nd Street have turned into commercial businesses," she said. "In the daytime it's alive--the street so full it's hard to find a parking spot. But at night it's quiet and peaceful."

One night, she said, the peace was disturbed by a not very bright burglar robbing Roe's plumbing business next-door.

"He was making a lot of noise by shoving things under the chain link fence onto the sidewalk," she said. She peeked out of her bedroom window and noticed a large white 'V' on the sleeve of the man's sweatshirt." A little later, as she was talking to the sheriff on the sidewalk the burglar drove right past them, she said, the white 'V' almost glowing in the dark.

"'That's him!" Valora shouted.

Because the sharpening shop is so friendly--an unfriendly Dalager would be about as unlikely as a cold-hearted Golden Retriever---it's become a sort of clearing house for people trying to track down friends and relatives who've moved.

"Every summer people come back to town for high school reunions and they troop in asking us where they can find such and such a person," Danny said. "We often get calls from City Hall, too, when they're trying to locate someone."

One night Danny even got a call--"A collect call" he said--from someone planning to sneak across the Mexican border.

"His relatives had moved. He didn't know where they were, and he needed them to come and pick him up," Danny remembered, adding that the man later got amnesty. "Some days we speak almost as much Spanish in the shop as English, because so many of the gardeners in this area are Hispanic."

Nearly all the Dalagers are fluent in Spanish. If they're gone when a Spanish-speaking customer comes in then Moses, their Hispanic mechanic, is usually around. Moses has worked with them for twenty three years.

"Moses is fun," Valora said. "Every week day he and I eat our lunch together while we watch the soap opera 'The Young and the Restless.'"

Before Grandma Lux's old house was moved to 2nd Street, Danny said, it used to be next-door to the saloon on South Coast Highway 101 that's now the Daley Double.

"It would have been nice to have preserved it as a part of local history," he said. "But if we hadn't pulled it down, that house would have fallen down by itself."

CHAPTER THIRTY SEVEN

"The Terwilliger Family, Horses, Dancing and Del Mar Roots"

Written December 1998

    Don Terwilliger was 6-years-old the day, in July 1937, his father took him to opening day at the Del Mar racetrack. He remembers his father perching him on top of a fence as they watched Bing Crosby (who took tickets at the gate that day) chatting to Dorothy Lamour.

"The thrill of seeing horses racing has never changed" Don said. "I haven't missed a season since--except once, when I was dancing in "The Music Man" and couldn't get back from Canada."

Don wasn't the only racing enthusiast in the family. His great aunt, Mae Kibler, Del Mar's Postmaster for thirty years, always made it to the track by 1 p.m. "She'd go to work very early," Don says, "And sit at her desk behind a post office manual with a racing form tucked inside."

The first Terwilliger to arrive in this area was Don's grandfather, Claude, who bought three hundred acres of Rancho Santa Fe, and built a ranch house there, in 1924. An entrepreneur, Claude Terwilliger bounced from project to project., Don said. "Walnut farming...horse trading...rodeo promoting. He'd say casually to my grandmother 'I've invited a hundred people to a barbecue this afternoon,' while she rolled her eyes upwards."

Claude's son Ted, Don's father, was a much quieter type. He'd a degree in horticulture, and was a landscaper when, in 1929, he married Louise Kibler (the bride rouged her knees for the occasion) in a house on Del Mar's Stratford Court. Unlike his quiet father, Don remembers his mother as "a small dynamo."

"Mom was star-struck," he said. "She went on Queen For A Day, when it was filmed at the Fairgrounds, and said her wish was that her son meet Fred Astaire so he could 'Get him into the movies'."

In 1942 Louise enrolled Don in Del Mar's earliest dancing school, which was also on Stratford Court. "The teacher, Mrs. Jefferson, was a former Miss Texas, beautiful, and only eighteen," Don remembers. "She used to roll her piano out of the garage and teach on the driveway, because there wasn't room in the house."

Although, he says, he showed no evidence of talent then—"I was a very small kid; in the toreador dance my cape was bigger than I was"--his starstruck mother kept trying.

In the early '40s Louise and Aunt Mae encountered director William Wellman in the bar of the Del Mar Hotel." Wellman was filming "This Man's Navy" at the blimp base beside the Fairgrounds. "At 2 a.m. Mom shook me awake," Don recalls. "'I've brought William Wellman home,'" she said. "'Get up! He's going to put you in movies!'"

Wellman didn't put him in the movies, but Don had other pleasures. Del Mar was so sparsely populated that he and his cousin, Carol Hasselo, left ropes permanently dangling in trees from 13th to 15th Streets and swung along them playing "Tarzan". Grandfather Terwilliger lent him horses to ride (Unfortunately he usually sold them just about the time Don grew attached to them.) But in 1946, when his father became grounds supervisor at the fairgrounds, Don was able to own a retired racehorse, Bonico, and stable him there.

It was also in 1946 that his parents bought a lot, and built a house, on 20th Street." $400 for the land, $1,500 for the house," he said.

In high school, at San Dieguito, Don was a kid who often walked around with a racing form under one arm, tap shoes under the other. His idols were dancers like Gene Kelly.

"Judge McLaughlin, who was both a guard at the racetrack and a local judge, used to let me into the empty Turf Club to practice," he said. "The roof leaked, and on rainy days I'd tap dance across the black and white tiles dodging puddles."

Don went on to dance professionally for twenty years, including seven in Las Vegas. He spent another twenty three in television sitcoms—"As a stand-in who also did bit parts" he said--with long runs on Rhoda, Cheers and Murphy

Brown. (He still gets residuals from saying a single word, "Moo", to a pregnant Murphy as she stepped out of an elevator).

These days Don, who is president of Del Mar's Historical Society, lives in a peaceful, Spanish-style house on the spot where his parents' house once sat. In racing season he goes to the track very early to wander around. "While the morning is still cool, and the steam rises from the horses coats as they're soaped after exercise," he said. "The smells never change. Warm horse flesh, alfalfa, the peppermint smell of liniment. Even the manure smells wonderful to me."

A few years ago he was in a television news spot, filmed at the fairgrounds. "On the wall behind me was a blown-up photograph of the crowd the first day of the races," he said. "At one point I turned around, and there we were--my father leaning on the fence, and my six-year-old self perched beside him.

CHAPTER THIRTY EIGHT

"Four Presley Brothers Remembered with Affection"

Written December 2000

    The year was 1942 and Betty Jo Truax, aged seventeen, was working after school in Encinitas Safeway.

    "Sugar and chocolate chips were rationed. You needed coupons to buy them," Betty Jo said. "I mentioned to Smitty, the manager, that Mom Presley and I wanted to make chocolate chip cookies to send to her boys."

    "Mrs. Presley?" Smitty said, "For her I'll find chocolate chips!"

    "Everyone in town knew that Mom Presley had all four of her sons in World War II," Betty Jo said. Russell was in Navy submarines, Frank a Marine

Corps pilot, Johnny a Navy pilot, and George a Marine radio operator on a bomber.

Betty Jo, who at nineteen was engaged to Russell--"As he was usually in a submarine I didn't see him very often"--dated Frank when she was only thirteen. "He was eighteen, but it was an innocent sort of dating," she remembers. "Movies at the La Paloma, making fudge at my sister Maxine's house, that kind of date."

Frank came to pick her up in an ancient Pontiac truck with mud flaps that slapped against the wheels. "We lived on the bluffs, north of the Self Realiztion Fellowship," she said, "Whenever my brother, Jim, heard Frank's truck he'd chant, "Here comes the flap, flap, flap of the Pon-ti-ac."

The Presley parents, Marine Corps pilot Captain Russell A. Presley (called Pop) and his wife, Mae, (Mom), moved to Encinitas in the '30s when Pop retired.

"Every Sunday afternoon, in their house on La Veta Avenue, Mom produced a feast," Betty Jo said. "All her sons enjoyed playing pranks. One Sunday I looked down into my vegetable soup and saw a rubber lizard."

She suspected, she said, George, the youngest, then eleven. "George had carried the soup in, and he seemed to be watching me intently." She was determined not to give him any satisfaction, she remembers, so she cut the rubber lizard in two with her fork, swallowed it, and exclaimed. "That was the best soup I ever had!"

Like numerous Americans the Presley brothers were the right age to be in both World War II and the Korean War.

"George was in two wars before he was twenty-five," remembers Marian Parker Presley, who married George in 1951; three weeks after he got home from Korea.

Johnny was actually the first Presley brother Marian met, in 1948. This was soon after she arrived in Encinitas, a 20-year-old girl from Minnesota, who'd come to work as a teller in the Bank of America managed by her uncle, Vern

Owens. The bank was next-door to the La Paloma, in the corner building that's now about to become Martini Ranch bar.

"It was a small, friendly bank," Marian said. "In those days the manager could approve a loan the same day someone asked for one."

There was no air conditioning in Encinitas then. On humid days a large ceiling fan spun above the customers' heads. "One day a man came in carrying a plank over his shoulder, and sheared off the fan blades," Marian said. "This happened twice!"

Johnny Presley worked at the bank between wars. "You should meet my brother, George," he told Marian.

Johnny had married the girl-next-door, Doris Mitchell, in '44. They already had a son and a baby daughter.

"When George came to pick me up he was driving Johnny's car, with the baby's seat still strapped on," Marian said. "I thought, oh oh, he's married."

On the day of their wedding George's brother Frank--by this time a highly decorated war hero who'd reached the rank of Major--lent them his shiny, new, black Buick convertible.

"We drove happily away to a honeymoon in San Francisco," Marian remembers. "Leaving Frank with my car--a battered old Ford that smoked if pushed past fifty."

Later, she said, they discovered that Frank stored all his medals in the Buick's glove compartment.

Johnny had reinlisted in the Navy by this time, so George and Marian rented Johnny and Doris Presley's house at 228 A Street, where the back door opened straight into the bedroom. (In a recent column about firefighters I mentioned a volunteer fireman called Poochie bursting into George and Marian's bedroom one night shouting, "Where's the nearest hydrant?")

"There were small houses on A Street, some are still there today, that I believe were built in the 1880s for the families of men working on the railway," Marian said. "There used to be a deep gully where Highway 101 is, and, on dark nights, the railway workers' wives hung lanterns on their porches to guide their men home."

Although it was unusual in the '50s, her brother-in-law Frank remained a bachelor at thirty-two, Marian said.

"I think every woman who knew him was half in love with Frank. He was stationed on the East Coast, but whenever he was home he'd head straight for Moonlight Beach."

In 1953 Betty Jo, by then married to a colonel in the Marines, had a visit from Pop Presley. "He told me Frank had got married to a dancing instructor," Betty Jo remembers. "'She's lovely,' Pop told me. 'Frank's very happy.'"

Only a few months later Betty Jo was sitting at her dressing table when she noticed her husband standing in the doorway with a strange look on his face.

"Dick said he'd some sad news to tell me about an old friend of mine," she remembers. After surviving two wars, and having his plane shot down twice, Frank had died in a peace-time accident on an aircraft carrier.

Footnote: If you're on the bluffs overlooking Moonlight Beach, between B and C Streets, Frank Presley's name is on one of the "memory benches". There are ten of these, each in memory of someone who, in life, loved Moonlight Beach.

CHAPTER THIRTY NINE

"Lauralie Dunne Stanton, Growing Up Next-door to Auntie Bath."

Written October 2000

    Lauralie Dunne had already been in one major earthquake when, in 1938, she moved to N. Cedros Avenue in Solana Beach. Six years earlier, when she was four years old and living in North Hollywood, she'd been trapped in a bedroom for nine hours.
    "When our house on Cedros began to tremble I was so terrified I ran screaming into the street," Lauralie remembered. "But it was only the train rushing past."
    The house Lauralie moved into when she was ten, with her mother, stepfather and 5-year-old stepsister, Jane, is painted pink and purple now and has

metamorphosed into Vintage Rose Antiques. In 1938 there was a grape arbor behind it, where damp spider webs brushed her face as she fed the ducks in the early mornings. There was a small guest house, too, flanked by Avocado trees, where Joe Hernandez, who announced the races at the Del Mar track for years, stayed during racing season.

"There were very few houses on Cedros," she said. "The Union Oil refinery was across the street west of us, the Standard refinery to the south." But they did, she said, have Auntie Bath living next-door.

"Auntie Bath was a little old lady who, every racing season, turfed her chickens out of their coops so that she could rent the coops to the track's trainers and exercise boys," she said. "They brought their own sleeping bags. Some of them slept behind her house in tents."

All through the racing season, Lauralie remembered, Auntie Bath would squirrel herself away in her bedroom, with a hot plate. "She'd have about thirty people living inside her two bedroom house, all paying her rent."

Those were the days, she said, when neither Solana Beach or Del Mar had a single traffic light, (Encinitas had one), and getting across Highway 101, especially in racing season, was "extremely difficult".

The local population was so small, money so tight, almost everyone had more than one job. "The principal at Solana Beach Elementary, Gordon Wells, was only about twenty-three," she said. "He taught 4th, 5th and 6th grades, and was also a life guard. And the head life guard at Fletcher Cove, Bill Rumsey, moonlighted as a bouncer at the Mission Beach Ballroom."

In 1941 Lauralie, at thirteen, got her first after school job at Solana Beach's drugstore, Dietrich's, on Highway 101. Her friends Joyce McKenna and Virginia Wilkens worked there too.

"Between us we ran the soda fountain, making numerous steak and egg salad sandwiches in the back kitchen, keeping the fudge for the hot fudge sundaes hot, and washing and drying all the dishes by hand," she said.

"Ruth Eischen, who paid our wages because she leased the soda fountain from Mr. Dietrich, baked incredibly good pies. The local people knew what time of day Ruth's pies would be ready and they'd be lined up at the counter."

It was while Lauralie was working at the soda fountain at Del Mar's drugstore, on the corner of 101 and 15th, that she became friendly with bandleader Harry James, and his wife, Betty Grable.

"They asked me if I'd babysit their two small children, in their rooms at the Del Mar Hotel," she said. "It was a perfect job, because the children were usually asleep, and I could sit there, in peace, and read."

As an added bonus she was allowed to bring a date, free of charge, to dance to the live music on the hotel's patio.

For the students of San Dieguito high school then dating usually began around thirteen or fourteen, she said. "We were like a big extended family. No matter where we lived, Solana Beach, Del Mar, Rancho Santa Fe, we were all bused to the same high school in Encinitas."

She remembers moonlight hay rides; the big wagon of hay pulled by rancher Herman Wiegand on his tractor. The girls went to slumber parties at the home of Barbara and Crix Ecke. Lauralie has vivid memories of their father, poinsettia pioneer Paul Ecke, Sr., standing in his kitchen, wrapped in an apron, making donuts for everyone.

"Mrs. Keogh, who owned the La Paloma movie theatre, was a widow with three sons, John, Jack and Al," she said. "They lived in the apartment over the theatre, and we'd have great parties there. After the movie was over we'd go downstairs and play hide and seek among the rows of empty seats."

By fifteen Lauralie was "sort of" engaged to Ralph Swaim, who was the youngest in a family of ten brothers and sisters, all of whom were gifted athletes.

"He was a junior life guard at Fletcher Cove," Lauralie said. "Every payday he'd buy red roses, and find a kid on the beach who'd deliver them to my house." She and Ralph used to dance to the big-band sound of Woody Herman's orchestra at the Mission Beach Ballroom on old 101. " There was no alcohol served, but we still had to lie about our age, and say we were eighteen, to get in."

Lauralie didn't marry the athletic Ralph, but another local star athlete, Bill Stanton, whom she met at the Oceanside/Carlsbad Junior College. (Now MiraCosta).

"During football games the girls played football at half time," she said. "And Bill coached us."

Longtime locals are most likely to remember Lauralie Dunne Stanton as a teacher at Cardiff Elementary. She was there for thirty five years, from '58 to '93.

"Mostly, I taught first grade," she said. "I figure I must have taught about 1,100 children to read."

CHAPTER FORTY

"Cory's Mercantile"

Written March 2000

— *This was an anniversary column as it was the one hundredth one published. The bicycle store mentioned burned to the ground in the fire of December 2000 that ravaged three stores on that block.*

If you're driving through Encinitas on the Coast Highway, you'll pass, on the corner of E Street, the building of American Print. Back in the '20s and '30s it was home to Cory's Mercantile--which sold everything from Stetson hats to ladies corsets to Wolverine work boots--and was owned by "Smiling Sam" Cory. (The nickname is mine. Every person I've spoken to who remembers Sam said he was "always smiling".)

Not that Sam, who emigrated from Lebanon as a boy of thirteen, always had reason to smile. On a night in 1935 thieves bashed a hole through one of the store's brick walls and took his entire stock.

"When he came in the next morning the only thing left were the fixtures," remembers Ed Cory, Sam's eldest son, who was twelve that year. "Dad had a shotgun, and he bought me a pistol. For several years the two of us slept on cots in the back of the store."

Eventually the merchants along that strip of 101 got together and hired a man called Woods as night watchman. "Woods patrolled on foot, testing locks, shaking doors," Ed said. "One night he got struck on the head, from behind, by someone who dashed into Sturdivant's Drugs and took several packets of cigarettes before Woods recovered consciousness."

Thieves, if caught, usually turned out to be transients. The locals, Ed emphasized, didn't go in for robbing each other in this small town where, like the bar in the television series Cheers, "Everybody knew your name".

In the early '20s Sam, whose original name was Shickrey Khoury (the five Khoury brothers voted to become "Corys" when they reached America) had been running a store with one brother in Gallup, New Mexico. "It wasn't working out," Ed said. "In 1924 Dad started exploring the coast. When he reached Encinitas he turned to my mother and said, 'Lily, we'll stop here.'"

Horse drawn wagons still clattered through town in those days. Model-Ts lined the curbs. "J. W. Rupe, who owned the general store, sold Dad apple boxes for a nickel each," Ed said. "And that's how he started--with apple boxes covered with neatly folded socks and underwear, set out on the sidewalk."

Within a year Cory's was an elegant, narrow store filled with clothing for men, women and children. It was the only place in town selling shoes.

"Sam himself was always smartly dressed, in a suit and a tie," remembers Bob Hernandez. In fact the only time Sam appears to have been without a tie was while bathing or sleeping. "He even mowed the lawn wearing a tie," Ed said.

Both Sam and his wife, Lily, loved talking to customers. Life moved at a slower pace then, and Ed remembers seeing customers drinking coffee with his parents--sitting on the chairs used for trying on shoes--deep in conversations that sometimes lasted for hours.

When the Depression hit Sam helped many of his customers struggle through on credit. "Some offered to barter, things like a sack of beans in exchange for a pair of pants," Ed said. "Dad would smile and say, 'Sure. I can eat those beans.' There was a guy who raised chickens on the hill above the shop. One day he came in and said his brother had died. He needed a suit for the funeral. 'I'll pay you in chickens,' he said. 'Week by week.' It got to the stage where I'd groan, 'Not again!' whenever dinner was chicken and beans."

"Sam Cory spoke fluent Spanish," Bob Hernandez remembers. (Sam had picked it up during his teens in New Mexico, where he delivered groceries to an Indian reservation that was so far out in the wilds he often had to stay all night.) "At one time practically the whole population of Eden Gardens shopped at Cory's." Bob said. "We shopped on credit--we'd no choice in the Depression--but Sam always looked delighted to see us. I remember my Dad lining us up in the store, explaining we needed shoes for school."

In the mid '30s Sam moved the store up the block to where the bicycle store is now. In 1950 Ed, and his younger brother, Leonard, took over. They renamed it Cory Brothers, moved up to Santa Fe Plaza and concentrated on men's clothing. Their second store was in Solana Beach, near the Jolly Roger restaurant.

One of my favorite anecdotes about the kind of merchandise Cory's Mercantile sold came from Marguerite Miller, granddaughter of Olivenhain pioneer Adam Wiegand.

"When grandfather died, in 1921, it was during a flood. The ground in Olivenhain's Pioneer Cemetery was thick mud," Marguerite said.

"I was five then. I stood in the rain, mother's hands resting on my shoulders, watching as my father, Alwin Wiegand, dug a grave with a shovel. Mud clung to the legs of his one good suit, but my mother said at least she knew his feet would be dry. Those Wolverine work boots were as waterproof as concrete!"

As this was three years before Smiling Sam Cory drove into Encinitas , Marguerite's father probably purchased his boots from the Sears Roebuck catalogue. Which was something everyone had to do before Cory's Mercantile opened.

CHAPTER FORTY ONE

"Maggie Zuerner Wolfe--a Life Filled With Firsts."

Writtten November 1998

Margaret Zuerner Wolfe--"Most people call me as Maggie," she said--has an unusual family history. It's filled with firsts.

They began, those firsts, in 1912, long before she was born. That was the year her 6-foot-4-inch grandfather, Walter Hyer, and her 5-foot grandmother, Clara, moved to Del Mar.

They lived, with their four musically-talented daughters, in a beach house named "The Sand Dollar" that Walter built on the north side of what is now 18th Street. It must have been quiet that first winter. They were the first year-round residents to live on that side of town. (First #1).

"The house is still there, near the power station," Maggie told me when I went to interview her. "Grandfather was always building something. He'd build a new house, move the family into it, sell their former home, do it all over again."

She opened the book, "Del Mar, Looking Back" to show me page 140, where, in a grainy 1914 photograph of the beach, nine houses he built are in the background. (They were Del Mar's first beach houses, so that's #2.)

If you're strolling around Del Mar you might see some of Walter Hyer's other homes. "The one at 410 15th St. known as the "Rock Haus", was one of his.

It looks as if rocks are embedded in the porch, walls and chimneys," Maggie said. (They're really slag bricks). "And all the houses on 15th that have an "English" look were his. I once asked my grandmother how many times she'd moved. She sighed and said, 'Margaret, I have no idea.'"

The Hyer's most exotic home, April Cottage at the junction of Zuni Drive and Forest Way, had sunken gardens that resembled a rain forest.

It was in the rain forest-like garden, in 1919, that Maggie's mother, Margaret Louise Hyer, (one of the four musical daughters), married Albert Wesley Zuerner.

"They met when mother, along with two of her sisters and a hired drummer they'd found through a newspaper ad, were playing at a Saturday night dance," Maggie said. "There's a photograph of my parents, taken right after their wedding, on page 185 of 'Del Mar, Looking Back.'"

I did a quick count and figured about 15 pages of the 304 page book referred, in some way, to her family. "It's the first time I've interviewed someone with this much material for reference," I told her. "So I'll make that #3."

Maggie's father was Del Mar's first electrician. (#4). He juggled this work with a second job as the town's first mail carrier. (#5).

"He'd go down to the train station and collect the mail about 8 a.m," Maggie, who was born in 1921, remembers. "He used his own pickup truck to do the deliveries."

Zuerner's route covered Sorrento Valley--"Just a few scattered ranches there then,"--Rancho Santa Fe, Eden Gardens, Solana Beach and Del Mar. "The population was so small that in the early 1930s he only had eighty mail boxes to cover. He got home by lunch time, and spent the afternoons doing electrical jobs, or selling ranges and hot water heaters out of the garage."

When Marston Harding used $150,000 of his cotton-mill fortune to build the Del Mar "Castle"--it was completed in 1927--Albert Zuerner did the electric wiring. Occasionally he took his 6-year-old daughter to work with him.

"He used to tell me that my child's hands were ideal for pushing wires through small spaces," Margaret said. "But I think he really wanted to give mother some time for her piano practice. I do remember pushing wires through to him, though, including some that led to the huge chandelier in the castle hall." (It seems a safe assumption that she was the area's first 6-year-old electrician's helper, so that's #6).

In 1934 Bing Crosby bought forty four acres of what had once been the Don Juan Maria Osuna ranch, on Via de la Valle. He built a house behind the original hacienda, and Albert Zuerner wired that, too.

"Bing's wife, Dixie Lee, loved my mother's piano playing," Maggie said. "I can remember coming home once in the late afternoon, walking up the hill to our house on Carolina Road, and hearing the music drifting down. When I got in Dixie Lee was sitting on the living room floor, listening. When Bing came over to drive her home he walked over to the piano and began to sing."

"The mail box at the Crosby's ranch was on my father's route. One hot summer day, in the school vacation, I was riding along with him, helping. I leaned from the pickup, opened the Crosby's box, and a cat that had been trapped inside flew out, straight through the window, into my lap. I've always suspected it was Gary, the oldest son, who put it there!"

That same summer, which was the year Maggie turned sixteen, she put on a white one-piece bathing suit and entered a contest held by the pool of the Hotel Del Mar. It was sponsored by Ann Sterrett, who owned the Del Mar Sportswear shop, and all the contestants wore bathing suits from the shop. "It was to pick Miss Del Mar," Maggie said, "who would later welcome visitors to the 1937 Fair, along with Miss Solana Beach and Miss Rancho Santa Fe. It was an early version of the Fairest of the Fair."

Maggie became--as I'm sure you've guessed--the first Miss Del Mar. (#7)

In her late teens she moved to an apartment in Rancho Santa Fe, because she was bookeeping for the market there. At lunch time she and a young landscaper named Clarence "Curly" Wolfe would meet behind the market to eat their sandwiches. They married when she was twenty, but, before that, Maggie achieved one more Del Mar first, bringing the total up to #8.

"When I was born there wasn't an Episcopal church in town," she said. "My parents never got around to having me baptized or confirmed."

In the late '30s plans for building a church were underway, but, as a temporary measure, a Realtor named Batchelder offered the spare room of his office on 14th Street. Maggie, aged seventeen, was the first Episcopalian to be both baptized and confirmed there.

"The room had an altar, and a railing, but it still looked like a real estate office," she said.

CHAPTER FORTY TWO

"Moonlight Beach Scene of Picnics, Parties and Laundry"

Written September 1999

    One of my favorite historical stories is about Moonlight Beach and grimy hotel guests. I found it in a small booklet, written by Annie Hammond Cozens, called "Brief History of Encinitas 1870 - 1950 ".

Late in 1883 Annie's father, Edward Hammond, built a three storey hotel in Encinitas. "To accommodate the growing population," Annie wrote. (During that year it had surged up to thirty five people.) The building is still there--Artistic Floors inhabits it--at 575 S. Coast Highway 101, although it only has two stories now. In its early years the hotel didn't have running water, but then neither did anyone else in the town.

"If a guest wanted to take a bath," Annie wrote, "He was invited to go to the beach, where all was free, and a bathing suit was not necessary, for he would be the only one there."

Edward Hammond had been a master cabinet maker in England. When he was building the hotel he celebrated getting the floor finished by sending word to all the neighboring ranchers to come to an all-night dance there.

"A dance in those days," Annie wrote, "Began with supper at dusk; then hot coffee--pots of it--sandwiches and cake about midnight; then dancing until dawn so that people could follow the meager roads back to their homes."

"About midnight the lights of the Southbound train were reported. All the bonfires were lighted, showing the surrounding wagons filled with sleeping children. The violin strains of "Gal on a Log" filled the air as old Tom Rattan, yellow whiskers pointed straight upward, sawed and stamped his loudest, and everybody danced his hardest."

Annie was thirteen when, along with her parents, six brothers and sisters, one grandfather, and her sister Jenny's fiancé, she arrived in Encinitas by train. It was February 1883.

They'd been expecting to see a picturesque village, nestled among orange groves. As the travel-weary Hammonds stared at the reality--four dusty buildings and not an orange tree in sight---they overheard the train's young, red-haired fireman saying to the engineer, "Another family of greenhorns come here to starve." His name was Tom Cozens. Six years later Annie's would marry him.

The Hammonds may have been temporary greenhorns, but they had money, and skills. Most of them also possessed musical talents. The ship that carried them from England also carried their elegant furniture, their china, their lead-lined piano. Edward , helped by his son, Ted, built a large hilltop home, "Sunset Ranch", where the east end of Leucadia Boulevard is today. Unfortunately, unless it rained, the nearest water was in a tank down by the Encinitas railroad crossing.

"Most any afternoon the younger girls of the Hammond family could be seen on the trail leading a horse loaded with a ten gallon supply of water," Annie wrote. "A wagon was not to be had in the neighborhood then."

In February 1884 they got too much rain, and the red-haired fireman's words about coming here "to starve" almost came true.

"The big floods came," Annie wrote. Several miles of train track were washed out. Encinitas was cut off from all sources of food supply. Ted Hammond, and one other man, Lemuel Kincaid, half rode and half swam to San Diego but, naturally, they were limited in how much flour they could carry back.

"The town was getting desperate," Annie wrote, although they were managing to shoot some game . Finally, a retired sea captain, "Cap" Hewson, struggled down to San Diego on horseback and arranged for a schooner to bring supplies.

"The ship hove in sight about two miles off shore--and stayed there!" Annie wrote. "Every resident of the community hurried down to the bluff. The crotchety old captain was fuming and frothing up and down, stumping along on his rheumatic legs. But the captain of the schooner was afraid to come in closer, or to send his boats in. For two days, while everyone stood on the bluffs, the supply ship lay off-shore beyond the kelp beds. There were no boats in Encinitas so the townspeople were helpless."

The schooner, accompanied by Cap Hewson's shouted curses, returned to San Diego. Three weeks later a train got through to Encinitas.

The Hammond Family tree records that Annie married her red-haired fireman, Tom Cozens, in 1889, and that their children were Harold, Bert and Kathryn. Tom became Encinitas postmaster and owner of the town's biggest dry-goods store . Later he owned, printed and edited the town's newspaper. Annie was on the Board of Trustees of the Encinitas and Carlsbad Unified School District.

The Cozens built a house overlooking Moonlight Beach. In 1900 they moved it nearer to Cottonwood Creek, to the place where it still stands, on the west side of Highway 101 across from the Encinitas Bazzar. (It's partially screened from the road by tall palm trees.)

But it's a single detail about the Cozens' house that usually intrigues people interested in local history. Using the water from the creek Annie and Tom became the first people in this area to have an indoor bathroom--with hot and cold running water.

CHAPTER FORTY THREE

"Lima Beans, Dust, Played Role in 1930s Romance"

Written February 2000

Susan Barrantes, explaining how her daughter Sarah Ferguson met Prince Andrew, once said, "They met on the polo fields. But then, doesn't everybody?"

If you happen to drive past Rancho Santa Fe Polo Club's fields, at the intersection of Via De la Valle and El Camino Real, you'll be passing the scene of a more local romance.

Back in the 1930s that land was covered by Alwin Wiegand's lima bean fields. And it was in those fields, in 1935, that romance flourished between Kay Candee and Richard Lyman.

Kay was a city girl. She lived with her widowed mother in Berkeley, and earned the substantial sum, (for that Depression year), of $125 a month working for San Francisco's City of Paris department store.

Richard was born in the North County, in an isolated farmhouse overlooking Batiquitos Lagoon. His father, Charles Lyman, had been a doctor before he became a farmer, which was convenient because he could deliver his own children. In 1935 Richard was twenty-three, a graduate of Davis Agricultural college, working with his father on the farm.

"Lima beans were about the only way you could make good money in this area then," Richard said. "Alwin Wiegand, who had the biggest farm in the area, owned a bean thresher and he went around and did the threshing for the smaller farms. That September my older brother, Jack, and I were helping Alwin harvest his own beans."

The land where today the hooves of polo ponies thud, and polo mallets thwack, hosted different sounds in '35. Work horses, in teams of four, hauled rattling wagons to the threshing machine. The warm, dusty air was full of flying chaff and the roar of the thresher's teeth splitting bean pods.

Jack Lyman's bride of three months, Pauline, was a close friend of Kay Candee's. "Come and spend your two-week vacation with us," Pauline urged Kay in a letter. The day Kay arrived Jack brought Richard home with him for dinner.

"That evening we walked on the beach," Kay remembers."The tide was low, the sand full of quicksilver. Every wave sparkled with mica."

"It was like having a private beach," Richard said. "It's the State Beach now, but back then my parents' farmhouse was the only building around."

The next day Kay went along to the bean fields. "I was driving a wagon, so she rode beside me," Richard said. "After a couple of times she could drive it herself, even the tricky part of maneuvering the beans onto a table in a net that was lifted by pulleys."

But what impressed him most, Richard said, was that this city girl wasn't bothered by the fact that she was covered in dust.

Lima bean threshing doesn't start before midday because the dew has to dry from the beans first. Each morning Richard and Kay rode horses into the hills, or along the beach.

One afternoon Herman Wiegand, Alwin's younger brother, watched Kay driving a wagon as he sat sewing beans into hundred-pound burlap sacks. "Richard, you'd better grab that girl," he advised.

Richard had reached that conclusion himself, but Kay's vacation was almost over. If he proposed, he wondered, would she accept him? "I asked her while we were riding on the beach," he said. "Much to my joy she said 'Yes!'"

Kay returned to San Francisco, to reply to her mother's "How was your vacation, dear?" with the news she was in love. And engaged!

"My mother was quite surprised," she said.

Richard worried that he wasn't earning enough to support a wife. But then P.W. Litchfield, founder of Goodyear Tire & Rubber, started a program to help young farmers who'd been to college "If you worked for him for two years," Richard said, "You were given the opportunity to own land in Arizona."

So Richard went off to Litchfield Park, an eight thousand acre farm in Arizona, and Kay kept working at the City of Paris. They wrote to each other every day.

"The San Francisco Bay Bridge was finished today," Kay wrote in 1937. "I walked across it, and then back again."

"I'm getting $60 a month at Litchfield Park, plus board and keep," Richard wrote to Kay. He managed to save enough from the $60 to buy her a diamond ring at Sears.

Finally, in February 1938, they were married. (Next Friday will be their 62nd wedding anniversary).

Richard decided not to farm in Arizona. "All summer long it was in the 100s" he said. "When we came back to Encinitas, in 1942, it felt like returning to paradise. We raised our five sons and our daughter here."

"Over the years we've often run into Herman Wiegand, who told Richard to grab me," Kay said. "Herman lived to be 103, and each time we met, he reminded me of those days in the bean fields."

CHAPTER FORTY FOUR

"Lucky Jack and his Fishing Family"

Written June 1998

    Jack Woolen's nickname isn't really Lucky Jack.
    "When I was a kid growing up in Encinitas they used to call me Smiling Jack," he said. I think of him as lucky, though. Ever since he's been old enough

to hold a cord with a horseshoe tied on one end of it (his inexpensive early substitute for a fishing pole) he's spent a large part of his life standing in the surf.

If you've ever fished the surf you know how exhilarating it can be: the soothing sound of the waves, the rhythmic massage of the sea swirling against your legs, the excitement when something--a mysterious something at first--tugs the end of your line.

Back in the '30s, when Bill and Emma Woolen and all seven of their children--four boys, three girls--used to clatter down the wooden stairs beside Swamis there was no limit to beach access. No rules existed about when and where you could, or couldn't, park. The only thing they had to worry about was the tide.

"It could be midnight, 2 a.m., 5 a.m. anytime," Jack remembers. "When the tide was coming in, down we all went to fish."

They didn't have far to go. All nine Woolens lived behind their store on Highway 101, at the south end of Encinitas; next-door to where "When In Rome" restaurant is today. The store was called "The Combination Market" because it sold a combination of things--groceries, flowers, fishing supplies and avacado ice cream. Jack, the baby of the family, was born in the apartment behind the store in November 1931.

Some of his earliest memories, when he was five, six, are of moonlight nights when he'd whirl his horseshoe around his head like a lariat before casting it into the sea. From the first, he said, he always caught something; although his 5-foot-2 inch Swedish-German mother--affectionately described by her family as "a fishing fool"-- often caught more fish then any of them.

On those nights, almost sixty years ago, the Woolens caught many of what Jack calls "the good eating fish" that are still around now--corbina, halibut, yellow fin, and spot fin croakers, who make a strange croaking sound like a hoarse dog. Occasionally a lobster would emerge, clinging to someone's bait.

After the fishing, Jack remembers, the family always enjoyed a feast.

"Our neighbor, Mrs. McClure, had a big combination kitchen-living room and a huge iron skillet," he said. "We'd take over a sack of potatoes, a sack of onions, and some of the fish we'd caught and she'd fry it all up for us, even if it was the middle of the night."

Any fish leftover went into the ice box. These were the pre-refrigerator days when Encinitas had an "Ice Man". His delivery truck held a great slab of ice ridged with notches, Jack said, "So he could hack off a block for each customer. Kids used to hang around while he hacked, hoping for ice chips to suck on."

Bill and Emma Woolen--who both lived to be ninety six--worked seven days a week in their store. As they sold a lot of bait Bill regularly loaded his sons into his Model T truck for bait-digging expeditions. The best bait of all, according to Jack, are rock worms. "If you use the head of a rock worm, it's almost impossible not to catch something," he said.

The rock worms, though, didn't exactly leap into the Woolen boys waiting hands.

"They're thick around as a ball-point pen, grow to two and a half feet, and they bite. We used to find them under rocks weighing several hundred pounds. All of us would get behind and push," he remembers.

As the Woolen kids married and had kids of their own, and the family grew, they still fished and camped together, driving their trucks along the North County beaches and parking right on the sand. (Which you could still do until the mid-'50s).

In 1978, more than forty years after he first whirled a horseshoe at Swami's, Jack won the World Marlin Fishing Championship. He won again in '81, and '90. This, of course, was deep-sea fishing, not surf, as marlins weigh hundreds of pounds.

"They're a thrill to reel in," he said. "They dance on top of the water. But no one needs that much fish to eat. Unless it's a trophy fish, or you're feeding a village, I strongly believe they should be tagged and returned to the sea."

If you're not a fisherman, but you think you'd enjoy an experience you might have had if you'd lived here hundreds of years ago, Jack recommends walking the Del Mar beach between 25th and 17th or 18th streets at high tide.

"Check a tide book, go down when it's coming in very early in the morning," he said. "Walk along the surf--not in it, you'll scare the fish--and you'll see corbina swimming past with their backs out of the water."

He's always happy to give fishing advice, Jack said. There's only one secret he'll never share--where to find those two and a half foot rock worms.

CHAPTER FORTY FIVE

"Growing Up in Eden Gardens"

Written June 1998

When I interviewed Bob "Chuckles" Hernandez we toured around the town of Eden Gardens in a van driven by his younger brother, Sam. This small town, where Bob was born in 1927, is a place many people see only in glimpses-- usually as they are parking to go into one of Eden Gardens' famous restaurants.

Bob Hernandez brought to life for me the smell of kerosene: the wind whistling through wall cracks, the traveling salesmen who came to town clutching catalogues and offering credit, and the cool, sweet taste of the chocolate vanilla bars sold at Pancho's Market. "You licked them all the way down to the stick because, sometimes, the exciting word "Free" was printed there," he said.

Seen through Bob's eyes Eden Gardens was, is, a community of families.

"That's where the communal showers and baths were," he pointed out as the van crept slowly along Ida Street. Only an empty lot remains now, half buried by a lush tangle of magnolia and apricot trees. "And see that little house there--that's where a barber cut hair for twenty-five cents."

When Bob was a boy the streets didn't have names. "We didn't need them," he said. "Everyone knew where everyone else lived."

Only about fifteen of the "original" homes are still there, mingled on the hillside with larger, newer ones. Eden Garden's two-room schoolhouse on Genevieve--where Bob met his wife Sara in first grade, and which used to overlook one of the Wiegand's lima bean fields--has vanished into a block of apartments. The wooden house on Vera street, the one painted the pink of Neapolitan ice cream, was once, Bob told me, used as the Protestant church. The Catholic church used to be two army barracks put together in a "T" shape.

"And that used to be Mr. Grenados' market," he said as we passed Don Chuy's restaurant on Valley Street. "Every Christmas a Del Mar man, whose name we never knew, sent silver dollars to the market to be handed out to any kid old enough to walk in. Sixty, seventy silver dollars, a lot in the '30s."

Everyone in Eden Gardens then belonged to one of about a dozen families, and almost everyone with a job worked for the fruit growers in Rancho Santa Fe.

"Particularly Ballard's" Bob said. "They paid every fifteen days, so people had to live on credit. On pay days you saw long lines paying in the markets, and the next day living on credit began all over again."

Two markets, and a roving grocery truck, served Eden Gardens in the '30s. Across from where Tony's Jacal now stands there was Panchos', a lively place that sold beer and had a pool hall. It had a gas pump, too, topped by a glass dome through which you could watch the gas coming down. When Bob was about ten Pancho paid him a quarter a day to come in early, before school, and sweep out the pool hall. This was where he discovered chocolate vanilla ice cream bars.

"After school I'd go back, with my cousin Dickie, and get two bars--they were a nickel each--and we'd sit and eat them on Pancho's wraparound porch."

Being a boy in Eden Gardens was, as Bob remembers it, lots of fun; although his father kept him home on Halloween nights so he couldn't join in the popular sport of tipping privies over.

"We were happy kids," he remembers. "We didn't know what we didn't have. When it rained the unpaved roads turned to mud, and we'd go watch cars struggling to get up Hernandez Street, only it didn't have a name then. We'd take bets on which cars would make it, which would slide back down again."

Another entertainment was making adobe bricks from Eden Garden's soil. "We'd stomp straw, soil and water with our bare feet," he said, "like wine-making."

The '40s brought changes. Twenty-three men out of Eden Gardens' tiny population, including Bob, went off to war and wider experiences. Then, in 1946, his Uncle Tony opened Tony's Jacal, in a two-room yellow house he'd inherited from his father. ("A very small house. 'Jacal' means 'little shack' in Spanish," Bob explains). Although no one had any idea at the time, Tony's Jacal, which started off so modestly that Tony kept his perishables in a Coca Cola ice chest on the floor, became part of several restaurants that were to draw people from all over the county to Eden Gardens.

In 1962 Bob, who worked as supervisor of the ground crew at the Del Mar Race Track for thirty-five years, bought a field on Genevieve Street, next-door to where his two-room school once stood. He built a large, comfortable house right over the ground where he played softball as a kid.

"My garage is where home plate used to be," he said. "One of the bedrooms is on second base. Apart from that one year in the Army, when I was eighteen, I've spent my whole life here."

CHAPTER FORTY SIX

"Blimps"

Written December 1999

    Readers of this column, to whom I'm eternally grateful, sometimes share stories with me in places like Home Depot. A reader I met in Von's market told me a story about sunbathing in the nude, in Del Mar, during World War II.

"I was in my back garden, completely surrounded by high hedges," she said. "I looked up to see a blimp from the nearby base hovering above the hedges. And the pilot was waving!"

Nowadays the Navy has replaced those enormous airships, known as "Lighter-Than-Air", with helicopters. But in World War II they were a vital part of defense for their ability to detect enemy submarines using M.A.D. (Magnetic Anomaly Detectors).

Del Mar's base was close to the fairgrounds, on land that today is partially covered by Interstate 5. Locals grew used to the sight of a 252-foot long, gas-filled bag crusising above the ocean. (A gondola underneath carried crew, fuel, equipment, and engines. And the bomb bay was underneath that.)

A few locals, though, regarded blimps as a menace.

"An inventor named Tippitt, and his wife, Ruth, who was an opera singer, lived in a mansion on ten acres of the bluffs across from where the Brigantine restaurant is now," Sid Shaw said. Sid, who flew blimps out of the Del Mar base, remembers it was almost impossible to get them to gain altitude quickly.

"We'd take off around midnight with a full load of bombs, and, engines roaring, barely skim the Tippitt's roof," he said. "Poor Mrs. Tippet was always calling the base to complain, with good reason."

Shortly before he was stationed there, Sid said, a blimp flew too close to a local farmer's turkey ranch and stampeded the birds. "The next day the farmer drove onto the base with a truckload of dead turkeys, demanding compensation."

After that, Sid remembers, an order was put out. "You will not fly over turkey ranches." Private back yards were also on the "you will not" list.

The bag part of the blimp nicknamed "The Poopy Bag", was filled with helium, the same kind of gas that keeps mylar balloons bobbing above childrens' parties. Blimps, of course, used considerably more of it; about 382,500 cubic feet.

Inside the bag two ballonets (small auxiliary air bags) kept the blimp's shape by having air either pumped into them or valved out.

"In the heat of the sun the gas expanded. And when you flew under clouds it shrank," said retired Navy Captain Alfred Cope of Rancho Santa Fe. (Captain Cope used to be my friend Harry's commanding officer, so I kept wanting to call him "Sir", but he asked me to call him Al.) "You couldn't let the pressure get too low because your blimp would look like a sausage."

Blimp pilots, Al said, trained in balloons attached to baskets. "The theory being that if your airship's engine ever failed at least you'd have had experience in free-ballooning." Helium was in short supply until the early '40s, he said, and the balloons of the '30s were filled with highly-flammable hydrogen. (The famous German Zeppelin airship The Hindenburg was using hydrogen when it burst into flames in 1937.)

"You couldn't take a radio up, in case of inflammatory sparks," Al said. "So we released carrier pigeons to let the base know our location. Not that we always knew it ourselves. We got lost over Amish country once. I leaned over the side and shouted "Where are we?" to a bearded fellow dressed in a big black Amish hat. He looked up, said, 'I see you up there!' and then ran back in his house, leaving us unenlightened."

"Free-ballooning was the greatest experience," former blimp pilot Harry Titus, of Oceanside, said of those training flights. "You'd almost no control. Except for altitude it was left to the gods. We used to drop torn-up pieces of toilet paper over the side to measure the altitude. If it went down we knew we were rising."

In Del Mar the wartime blimp base was a small one. "Usually only one blimp was kept there," Sid Shaw said. "It was tethered outdoors, because there wasn't a hanger, and someone had to stay with it twenty four hours in case it slipped its moorings and drifted away."

By the time Sid was stationed there it was June 1945. Germany had just surrendered, but Japanese submarines were still considered a threat to the vulnerable West Coast.

"We flew two hundred, three hundred miles out to sea, often patrolling for twenty four hours, midnight to midnight," Sid said. "We flew in bad weather because that was when submarines came up to charge their batteries."

By August 14th Japan had surrendered, but Sid stayed on the base until February 1946. He was privileged, he said, to be one of the pilots who flew "Greeter Hops".

"We took the bombs out of the bomb bays and installed speakers," he said. "As the aircraft carriers bringing service men back from the war sailed into Long Beach I'd fly out there, with performers like Peggy Lee and Dinah Shore singing to welcome them home. The real Peggy Lee, and Dinah Shore, not just their recorded voices."

Several hundred blimp pilots, including Sid, Harry and Al, still meet for biannual reunions. Harry put out their newsletter--"The Poopy Bag Ballonet"--for seven years, so I asked him how blimps got their name.

"There are many stories, probably none of them true," Harry said. "One version is that a Britisher once punched a finger into the side of a blimp and said, ' By jove, that feels limp,' "

FORTY SEVEN

"Jay Harold and Babe On the Saturday-Crowded Sidewalk"

Written March 2000

When Frank Sinatra sang about Saturday night being the loneliest night of the week he certainly wasn't singing about downtown Encinitas in the '20s and '30s.

"Almost everybody came to town on Saturdays," Jay Harold Williams said. "The stores stayed open until ten, eleven at night, just as long as there were any customers around."

The families from remote farms always came in on Saturdays, he remembers; people who perhaps hadn't talked to anyone all week but to each other and the occasional traveling salesman. "Saturdays were getting-together days, a chance to talk to the friends you met." As dusk fell street lights bloomed, and savory smells drifted from The Mint Cafe on the Southwest corner of D Street.

In the early 1930s Jay Harold and his younger brother Babe, (Babe's name was really Earl, but no one ever called him that), spent Saturdays at Shancks Feed & Grain Store where their father, Day Williams, worked sixty to eighty hour weeks for $18 to $25.

"In the late afternoons we'd stand outside the store and smile hopefully at Mr. Matthews, the manager of the La Paloma Theater, as he walked past on his way to work," Jay Harold remembers. "The theater charged ten cents for kids under twelve, but, occasionally, Mr. Matthews gave us movie passes."

Fred Shancks, who owned the feed and grain store--and two other Shancks Stores, in Oceanside and Vista--was the boy's step-grandfather. It was Fred who persuaded the Williams family, originally from Iowa, to move from South Dakota.

"The winter I was born was 40 below, so I don't think my mother and father needed much persuading," Jay Harold said. Day and Mary Williams arrived, with Jay Harold, three, and Babe, one, in 1927. In 1931, when the area was reeling from the Depression, Mary discovered that buying a house on Cardiff's Montgomery Avenue would be cheaper than paying rent. When they moved into 2051 it was the only house on the east side of the block. Fields of sugar cane grew on the south end.

"Cardiff was considered a poor area," Jay Harold said. "It was beautiful! The hillsides were covered with golden poppies. Thick pepper trees, planted by the town's founder Frank Cullen, shaded the 50-foot corners." With their collie dogs, Primo Carnera and Max Baer--- "Dad was a big boxing fan,"--the boys roamed freely. The sage brush along Montgomery was so dense they had secret places where they could hide standing up.

Hoboes camped, hunkered around their fires in a hollow near the railroad tracks. They made Mary Williams uneasy when they appeared at her back door, but she always fed them. "Usually an egg sandwich," Jay Harold said. "We kept chickens, and a goat. The Archers across the street kept a cow. Cardiff was rural then."

It was also a close-knit community. So close-knit that The Little Church of the Roses on Birmingham Drive welcomed everyone."Methodist, Catholic, Presbyterian--it didn't matter," Jay Harold said. Encinitas and Cardiff could only afford one minister between them, so on Sundays he shuttled back and forth.

When Fred Shancks died in 1937 his son, and son-in-law, inherited his stores and sold them. From then until the early '40s, when Day Williams went to work building B 24s at Convair, the family's finances often tottered along.

"We tried breeding rabbits," Jay Harold remembers. "At one time we had five hundred, in hutches behind the house. But most of them caught the disease Coccidiosis."

Day worked at the Union Station in Solana Beach when gas was eleven gallons for a dollar. He sold orange juice extractors at the San Diego Exposition, and ice cream at Del Mar's first two County Fairs. "At the first fair, in '36, it rained heavily," Jay Harold recalls. "Fairgoers had to reach Dad's stall across a plank over mud. My mother worked in Cardiff's Post Office, and Babe and I picked fruit after school, and sold magazines, going door- to-door to collect for Saturday Evening Post, Liberty, and Ladies home Journal.

"Dad's best job before the war was selling '38 and '39 Chevrolets for Harry Bunyard. The '39 model, at $1,300, was loaded with extras, like a heater, a radio, and side view mirrors."

In 1956 Jay Harold built a two-storied house on the corner of Montgomery and Birmingham, keeping one of Frank Cullen's original pepper trees to shadow the front yard. (It still does). "My mother, widowed by then, lived with me," he said. "When I got married in 1960, she built the house next-door." When she died, at ninety-four, Mary Williams had lived on the same Cardiff block for sixty five years.

The downtown Encinitas building, a block south of the La Paloma, that once held sacks of grain and live baby chicks when it was Shancks Feed and Grain, has turned into Dan's Coast Cyclery. But Jay Harold and his wife, Wanda, still live on Montgomery Avenue, only a few miles from where he and Babe waited hopefully for Mr. Matthews on the Saturday-crowded sidewalk.

CHAPTER FORTY EIGHT

"Lola's Double Life"

Written November 1998

It was the posters that drew Lola Roach's maternal grandparents, the Gayharts, to Leucadia. Distributed all over Los Angeles in 1928, they urged people to " Grow avocados in beautiful North County. Live the good life!"

"By the time they discovered what hard work it was, they owned a house and five acres on Union Street, " said Lola, who lived with her grandparents all through grade school because Los Angeles, where her parents lived, aggravated her asthma.

"Central school was only a few blocks away. I used to walk there with Paul Ecke, Jr.," she remembers.

Lola, however, was doing something that the other 6-year-olds in her class were not. Her uncle, Hal Roach, was a famous producer-director; whose work ranged from serious movies such as "Of Mice and Men " and "The Little Foxes", to the Laurel and Hardy and Charlie Chaplin comedies. Several times a year Lola would be whisked off to Hollywood to the Hal Roach Studio, which was actually in Culver city, to act in one of "The Little Rascals" films.

"Not that there was much acting required in my first job," she said. It was in "Cradle Snatchers", a film in which The Little Rascals, a gang of mostly good-hearted kids who were always in trouble, were supposed to be taking care of a baby. "I was the baby, nine months old, and appeared careening down a hill in a runaway baby buggy."

Lola's paternal grandparents lived in a house on the studio lot. "My grandmother always hung her washing out on a line to dry," Lola said. "So often the first thing people saw when they came in the studio gates was a line of flapping laundry."

Grandfather Roach managed the studio's finances. His elder son, Jack, Lola's father, was both a cameraman and a location scout. In the '30s, Lola remembers, action scenes required ingenuity.

"When my uncle was making "Captain Caution", with Ronald Coleman, it contained the difficult scene of a big sea battle, " Lola said. "Dad went out and made friends with a group of strong, healthy life guards at Santa Monica Beach.

A huge tank, filled with models of battleships was set up in the studio, and the lifeguards swam underwater and moved the ships around."

Working on The Little Rascals was fun, she said. "There was no script. Nothing written down. 'Do what you feel like,' my uncle would say, so the kids made it up as they went along." (And, in case you're curious, Alfalfa's straight-up-in-the-air cowlick was done by his mother.) Lola was in only about half a dozen of the "rascals" films, but was known as the one with the fair curly hair to whom the "bad boy", played by Tommy Bond, sang love songs." I was only about five, or six, but I can still remember him crooning 'I'm in the mooood for loooove.....,'" she says.

"One day Shirley Temple's mother brought her to the studio looking for work. 'Sorry, we already have one of those types with curly hair,' my uncle told her. And for the rest of his life--and he lived to be 104--he used to reminisce about how he'd lost out on Shirley Temple because of me!"

Life in Encinitas was interesting, too. Grandmother Gayhart was an avid boxing fan. Both grandparents took breaks from caring for the avocados to take Lola to the open-air boxing matches held downtown. "They were on a raised stage next door to where The Daley Double Saloon is now," she said. "Sometimes they'd have a professional fighter challenging all-comers for $10. That was a lot of money in the Depression."

Lola's asthma disappeared as she grew older, and her junior high and high school years were spent back in Los Angeles, living with her parents. By this time Grandmother Roach had taken to playing bridge on the deck of the Tuna Club on Catalina Island. "She used to take my sister and me along, then forget she had us with her," Lola remembers.

It was on Catalina island, when she was sixteen, that Lola noticed a tall, blond college student playing a pinball machine. " I thought he was gorgeous!" she says of Eric Larson, a 21-year-old pilot who was the son of Swedish immigrants. "He asked me to a dance that night at the casino, which cost ninety-six cents and included a free fruit drink."

When they'd been married for thirteen years and had three children, Eric and Lola Larson bought the house on Union street from her grandparents. "It's named "Union" because it's on the border between Encinitas and Leucadia," Lola said. "We love the place. Our fourth child was born here, and we've now been here forty-two years. "

The Larsons are movie buffs, and go often, but the writhe-about-naked sex scenes shown now would, Lola says, have sent most audiences in the '30s into shock.

"When I was about 16 I went, with a boy-friend, to see "George Washington Slept Here," she said. Part of the plot was that the two stars, Jack Benny and Ann Sheridan, accidentally sat on a bed together, before leaping apart. "My boy-friend and I were so embarrassed by an unmarried couple doing this, when we got outside we could hardly look each other in the eye."

Last March the La Paloma Theatre in Encinitas celebrated seventy years of showing movies. A reporter from Channel 51 came down to interview Irene Rupe Swoboda, who was the La Paloma's first cashier, and also Lola. "I've got a couple of clips of you," the reporter told her.

"When we got home I turned on the 11 'O Clock News," she said "And there I was, in black and white, tap dancing energetically behind Spanky MacFarland.

" I always tell people it wasn't talent that got me into movies, but nepotism because of my famous uncle."

In 1992, when Hal Roach reached 100, the Smithsonian feted the man responsible for the comedies of Chaplin and Harold Lloyd. A lot of countries in Europe wanted to fete him, too There was, naturally, concern about the rigors of travel at his age. Did he feel like going? To France? To Germany? To Italy?

"Uncle Hal not only went with enthusiasm," Lola said. "He took his girlfriend along, too."

CHAPTER FORTY NINE

"The Coles of Cole Ranch Road"

Written October 1998

When I first saw the 1911 photograph of Clarence Cole with his wife and three sons I thought, mistakenly, it was a photograph of a rich family.

There they all were, frozen for posterity inside an oval frame, in a copy of Richard Bumann's book "Colony Olivenhain" I found in Cardiff library. Clarence, his sons Arthur, five, and Henry, four, are in suits and floppy ties. Dark-eyed Amanda Cole, with baby Edward on her lap, looks, with her high lace collar, as attractive as a modern-day actress. (Demi Moore springs to mind.) You could picture Amanda drinking afternoon tea.

She could hardly have spared the time. Her grandson Stanley (Arthur's son) told me she worked backbreaking hours on a hundred acre farm near Olivenhain's Lone Jack Road. The family, now, always refer to it as "The Old Place".

Both Clarence and Amanda came from Olivenhain pioneer families who settled there in the late 1800s.

"But Clarence really didn't want to farm in Olivenhain," Stanley Cole says of his grandfather. "One time he loaded the whole family into a wagon and told them they were going to live in El Centro. But it rained so hard they got stuck in the mud and turned back."

Clarence's next move was to Chowchilla. His eldest son Arthur, always called Art, was about twelve when Amanda rounded up her three boys and told them, "I'm staying in Olivenhain. If you help me to work the farm, and pay off the mortgage, this land will be yours."

"It wasn't easy," Stanley said. Amanda sold her cream and butter to The Stratford Inn (which later became the Del Mar Hotel). She delivered it herself, rattling all the way from Olivenhain to Del Mar in a horsedrawn wagon. The Cole boys juggled school with farm work, raising lima beans, oat hay and black-eyed peas.

In 1922, when Art was sixteen, he earned extra money by opening a clay mine--a half mile northeast of Lone Jack Road--with two older friends, Alex Reseck and Fritz Wiegand. The three of them hauled out fifty tons of clay every day for months.

Many long time residents remember Art Cole as cheerful, good-natured and usually seen wearing a large-brimmed hat (except when he was riding his Yamaha motorcycle). He was the only one of Amanda's sons who stayed on the farm.

He didn't just farm, though. From the mid-'20s to the late '80s, Art was the local "tractor man". No one is sure just how many tractors he had parked around the farm, but Lynwood Cole, his youngest son, guesses the number at fifteen. "Two or three working, and the rest for parts," Lynwood remembers.

If anyone's vehicle got stuck in mud, flood water, or whatever, Art would turn out at any hour to rescue them. On one November day of torrential rain, in 1965, he hauled four cars and a tractor out of flood water, and then went back to pull a Mashburn garbage truck from a mud hole. "Sure was a mess" he wrote in his diary.

Art did remove his broad-brimmed hat the day, in 1941, he married Bertha Nesvold in the Methodist minister's home at the bottom of Cardiff's Birmingham Drive.

"An Encinitas barber, Al Johnson, took our wedding photographs," Bertha remembers. "He did photography as a sideline."

Art took his bride home to "The Old Place", to 4-year-old Art, Jr. (usually called Denny), his son from his first marriage. Amanda still lived on the farm, but she had her own small house.

"The Old Place" still didn't have anything in the way of modern conveniences. At night it was a lit by oil lamps, which looked picturesque but were hard work to clean. There was no electricity, indoor plumbing or running water. Amanda had always done the family laundry by scrubbing it vigorously on a washboard. Every Sunday Art drove a wagon into Rancho Santa Fe and hauled back enough water to fill the wooden cistern on the hill.

Fortunately Bertha had grown up on a farm in North Dakota. She was able to joke about the fact that her toilet was 100 feet from the back door. "The path from the farm to the outhouse was so well-used I told people we had 'five rooms and a path'," she said. By 1945 she also had a toddler, Stanley, a baby, Lynwood, and a Maytag washing machine.

"It had a gas engine, so I had to pump a pedal to start it," she said. It was a process rather like juicing up a motorcycle. Bertha pumped, the engine varoomed into action, and made so much noise she had to keep it outside.

In 1959 the Coles heard that a farm they liked, on fifteen acres half a mile south of them, was going to be auctioned for unpaid taxes. They moved there in 1960, and soon afterwards their lives changed dramatically. Olivehain had piped-in water!

The orchard produced so much fruit, Bertha remembers, that Art kept turning up in the kitchen with bucket after bucket of pears, plums and peaches. "One year I canned 100 quarts of peaches. They looked so attractive, all in shining rows, that whenever we had company Art used to take them on a tour of the canned fruit!"

When the neighbors voted to name the street "Cole Ranch Road" Art wrote in his diary that he was "real pleased about that". He died in 1991, but Bertha still lives on the farm with Lynwood, who combines caring for a herd of two hundred and twenty five "mother" cows with doing mechanical repairs. Stanley, who lives half a block away, also juggles two jobs--it seems almost a Cole tradition--as he took over his father's tractor work while keeping his job at Unisis.

"Dad worked hard all his life. He was still doing tractor work when he was eighty two," Stanley said.

Lynwood remembers standing on Rancho Santa Fe Road watching as his father towed a pioneer's wooden shanty the half mile from Marie Wiro's land to a spot beside the Olivenhain Meeting Hall. (You can still see the shanty there today.)

"He was always proud to say he was born and raised in Olivenhain." Lynwood said. " He knew every inch of the place."

CHAPTER FIFTY

"Visitors Survive Strong Dose of North County History"

Written May 2000

    Dave Young once remarked, in the back room of the San Dieguito Heritage Museum, that if you're enthusiastic about local history you have to be careful not to give visiting friends an overdose. "There's a point," Dave said, "at which their eyes start to glaze."

Recently, I had a couple of English cousins staying with me. I tried watching their eyes for signs of imminent glazing, but this area's past intrigues me so much I probably got carried away.

"Bing Crosby had a hunting lodge near here," I said happily as I drove them along Leucadia's Hillcrest Avenue. "It's in that little cul-de-sac; the old house on the end. He used to have Hollywood friends--like Jack Benny--down, and they hunted with hound dogs that bayed in the dawn, a blood-chilling noise that sounded like the Hound of the Baskervilles."

On Cardiff's Manchester Avenue I pointed out the "Dynamite House" (currently The Sculpture Garden), and explained how the farmer who lived there in the '30s sometimes blew up half a field if the mood was on him. Being English they weren't exactly dazzled by the house being over 100 years old, but something Mary Ann Wiegand Wood told me--that it was built by a 17-year-old boy--did impress them.

" When Mary Ann and her husband, Jim, bought the Dynamite House, in 1946, she found a mysterious jar of black pellets in the basement," I told them. "She thought they were probably some kind of blasting caps."

In old downtown Encinitas I got the chance to share my favorite local anecdote.

"Right there, on Highway 101--near the La Paloma Theater," I exclaimed, flinging out a hand to point to the theater "The local sheriff pulled over a speeding car and discovered Douglas Fairbanks, Sr. inside. He was driving around in the nude." (That story comes from the history trivia collection of Big Joe Gooding, one of the original Del Mar Terrace Rats).

In Douglas Fairbanks, Jr.'s book "The Salad Days" he wrote that his father was extremely proud of his body. To keep in shape for such silent movie feats as swinging from chandeliers he performed, in the nude, a series of muscle flexing exercises every morning in front of a mirror. If someone came to the door while he was exercising he would hold one hand over the part of his body modesty deemed should be covered, and keep the other hand free for opening the door.

I also told my cousins about the "Avocado Land Rush" of the '20s; and how people from other states were coaxed to this area by posters proclaiming, "Grow Avocados in beautiful North County. Live the good life!"

"The ones who came were put up in tents on the beach," I said, "and fed avocado ice cream while they listened to sales pitches."

My cousins didn't stay long, only two days. (This, I'm convinced had nothing to do with deluging them with local history. They were visiting us on their way back from a conference, and had to get back to work.) If they come again, though, I'd like to take them on a historical "wistful wander" through Solana Beach. The Wilkens brothers lent me a charming piece their mother, Florence, wrote about Solana Beach businesses in the '20s; when no one in town owned a telephone. Those businesses sound so friendly, so....unrushed.

"There was seldom more than one customer there ," Florence wrote of Col. Ed Fletcher's bank, which was on the northeast side of the Plaza. And only one employee was ever seen, a Mr. Bernie Ferguson. "He was able to take the time to make out each customer's deposit slip."

The post office, next door to the bank, sounds equally customer-friendly. Mrs. Waits, the postmaster, and her husband, lived in the back and ran an early version of a 7-11 in the lobby

"Mr. Waits used a wheelbarrow to carry the mail to and from the railroad tracks," Florence wrote. As the post office, like the bank, was about ten steps above the sidewalk he and the wheelbarrow careened down a steep cement ramp whenever he set off.

"It was quite a sight to see him pushing it across Highway 101 for at least four round trips a day," Florence recalled.

Solana Beach didn't have a railway station then, so mail was flung from a train passing through. For outgoing mail Mr. Waits simply hooked it onto a post, and the train conductor leaned out and grabbed it.

This tiny coastal community--in 1925 only thirty families lived in Solana Beach--had a blacksmith, a lumber company, two restaurants, two barber shops, two drugstores, a hotel, a real estate office, a Ford Agency and a grocery-dry goods store. Every Saturday night the Ford car dealer would move all his cars out into the street so the locals could come in and dance.

But the strangest thing about the town of Solana Beach in the '20s, I think, is the duplication of names. Among those thirty families were two sets of Wards, Wilsons, Kings, Carpenters, Baths, Davises, Stephens, Browns and Hunts.

"The telephone finally came to Solana Beach in the early '30s," Florence Wilkens wrote. Her husband, Duke, was asked to choose his own number.

What did he pick?

As any sensible person would, he chose 1-2-3.

AT THE END....

Mac Hartley, my fellow teacher at MiraCosta College, wrote a wonderful local history book--"Encinitas History and Heritage"--that came out just before Christmas in 1999. (History books, of course, never go out of date!) Near the book's end Mac wrote, "After the party is over there is always that lingering question. Who did I forget? I hope they will forgive me."

Words seem inadequate when it comes to thanking all the people who have allowed me to interview them, or have helped me with information for
The Backward Glance columns.

The column has had three North County Times editors: Teresa Hineline, Jose Sanchez Jr., and Janet Lavelle. All three have been supportive, warm, and encouraging. And all three of them have (fortunately, as they had to work with me) a great sense of humor.

My friend Sharon Bouchard volunteered to do this book's copy editing. Sharon's husband, Dick, who is a computer instructor, unraveled the mysteries of just what it was that Infinity Publishers wanted on the manuscript disks.

And it was another friend, Irene Kratzer, who, when I started the column, thought of calling it "The Backward Glance".

Being a Northern English woman, I'll revert to the language of my youth and simply say to all those of you who played a part in Backward Glances Vol. 1

THANKS , LUVS--YOU'VE BEEN SMASHING!